TALES *of the*
PEACEMAKER

THE FIRST PEACEMAKER
MERTH ANN'S VIEW

ASHLEY-LYNN HALL

Library of Congress Control Number	2021909909
Paperback	978-1-63626-078-5
Hardcover	978-1-63626-079-2
eBook	978-1-63626-080-8

Printed in the United States of America

Harrison Street, Hoboken
New Jersey, 07030
www.paperchase-solution.com
+1-800-850-2688

table of contents

CHAPTER ONE: **Who I Am**..1

CHAPTER TWO: **School Days** 3

CHAPTER THREE: **Races**..7

CHAPTER FOUR: **Exploring** 9

CHAPTER FIVE: **Guardian Encounters** 11

CHAPTER SIX: **Thinking Space and a Sea Dragon** 13

CHAPTER SEVEN: **Birthday Celebration**.......................................15

CHAPTER EIGHT: **Loneliness and Boredom**.................................19

CHAPTER NINE: **Exploring Further**..21

CHAPTER TEN: **Water Help**...25

CHAPTER ELEVEN: **Friend**..27

CHAPTER TWELVE: **Council Meeting** 31

CHAPTER THIRTEEN: **Meeting Dry People** 35

CHAPTER FOURTEEN: **Red Water**...41

CHAPTER FIFTEEN: **New Mers**......................................47

CHAPTER SIXTEEN: **Council United to See What I Saved Another From**......................................55

CHAPTER SEVENTEEN: **Warrior Clan Has Pain**......................59

CHAPTER EIGHTEEN: **Hurting a Jerk… Again**......................63

CHAPTER NINETEEN: **Group Rotations**......................67

CHAPTER TWENTY: **Memories and Feelings Not Mine**......75

CHAPTER TWENTY-ONE: **Removal of a Forced Document**.....79

CHAPTER TWENTY-TWO: **Forgiveness**......................85

CHAPTER TWENTY-THREE: **Feeling Alone**......................91

CHAPTER TWENTY-FOUR: **Guardian Without Gender**..........93

CHAPTER TWENTY-FIVE: **Buying a Human Debt**....................95

CHAPTER TWENTY-SIX: **Mer Jail Cells**......................105

CHAPTER TWENTY-SEVEN: **Good Information**......................109

CHAPTER TWENTY-EIGHT: **Wedding**......................111

CHAPTER TWENTY-NINE: **Learning and Sharing of Magic**..131

CHAPTER THIRTY: **Children**......................145

CHAPTER ONE

Who I Am

I am Merth Ann. I have olive toned skin, bright blue eyes and long black hair. I am the only child of King Merco Mer and Queen Meera Mer. I am therefore the heir to the nation. I learn things I suppose most children learn about and some things I am sure most do not know. Things I learn are the mer language, the magic common language, swimming with my tail and walking with my legs.

Other things I learn about are sea animals, such as fish and sharks, and sea plants such as coral and seaweed. I learn how to use my magic to communicate with other mers and sea life. I learn to spell, write, read, math, science, and mer history. Then I have lessons on etiquette, ruling a nation, contracts, alliances, and getting the sea life to obey me as needed. That was stressed as an only as needed in bad situations. Father used his commanding tone on that so I would not dare to disobey.

I learn about our laws and why they were put into place. I also learn the boundaries of the nation and how to tell if I get near our boundaries. No one remembers what is pass them besides lots of water if anyone ever knew. I wonder about that but am careful not to ask to many questions concerning it as it makes people annoyed when they do not know what you want to know. It makes them feel stupid. At least someone told me such. I guess it makes since. I do not enjoy feeling stupid.

Our laws are set up to protect us. Most you do not need to know. I will tell you magic common laws and what I know about them. One law is all promises must be kept. This is to make sure the magic nations can be trusted. Second law is bowing is freely giving up freedom, only if you do so willingly does that happen. It prevents forced slavery. Third one is first kiss between a couple when both freely give it is their marriage. I guess that is to make us choose carefully who we allow so close to us. Anyways, enough on that. Most find laws boring. I sure do. Knowing them and following them are good but learning them is bland.

CHAPTER TWO

School Days

As I follow my history teacher today, I see most mers only have one child. Very few have a second child, and it is almost unheard of for twins. Forget more then two children. I ask why that is. Teacher says, "I am not entirely sure. I suppose it is so that we do not over crowd our good ocean."

That make some since. If we populated faster than that, it could get crowded fast. However, that means that we about half the number of mers every year does it not? I voice my question. Teacher snaps at me to pay attention to what our lesson is about not letting my mind wonder. I guess she was feeling annoyed she could not give me an answer. I see my classmates want to laugh that I was the one punished not them, but they do not dare as I am their princess. BLAH! I never asked to be born a royal.

One of my class asks how long we could live. Teacher replies, "Most live three thousand years. A few of us have lived five thousand years, of course the majority of those were royals. Our magic prevents us from physically changing past our eighteenth birthday, keeping us healthy, strong and good looking."

The day continues. The afternoon is boundary lessons. Those my age of five and these that are age six are in one class. We swim to the boundaries. It takes us two hours. The water is dark here. Teacher tells us that every hundred feet is a fish we should not look at the light it puts off as we would become unaware of how close we were to it. A classmate asks how that is. Teacher has us stay in a tight group and follow him.

We do. I am at the back because I know they will need sense put back into them. I had seen drawings of this fish. It is called an Angler fish. I find it to be creepy. The light it gives off on the tip of its one antenna is inches from its mouth. By the time you realize what you are near it could be too late. They protect the mer boundaries. Teacher stops and turns partly back to us. Moments later, there is a bright light about twenty feet behind our teacher. I blink and widen my sight to take in the creepy looking fish. My classmates do not. They swim closer wondering about the light. Teacher smirks. I realize he is going to let them get a severe fright to make sure they pay attention in the future, but I cannot endanger my people so. I command, "Stop!"

My classmates stop. They do not dare disobey my commands. They wonder why I forced them to stop as they all look back at me. Teacher says, "Now class if you turn slightly but not fully, you will see why she made you stop."

The class slowly turns. As soon as they see the creepy fish, they scurry behind me. I am unafraid as I swim right next to it. I ask to see what it has experienced in the past week. It touches its antenna to my forehead. I see it eat half a school of fish in one setting. That overwhelms my class and our teacher. I quickly block the knowledge put off I do. I see other things including that it has three young offspring nearby. Once it shows me its past week it mentions it was looking forward to scaring the foolish mers. It was disappointed I did not let it mess with them. I shrug, it is my duty to protect my people the best I can. Then this fish says, "Little Mer Princess, I could eat you if I wanted to."

My class quickly tells me to get away from the strange thing. I ignore them because I have no reason to fear it as they do. I state, "Do you think my parents would let you get away with such? I figure they could eliminate your species on the desire to. I even get hurt would give them reason to do so."

It says, "A mild joke Princess. I was joking with you. None of us would dare harm you. The others though might make a tasty treat."

Knowing it is joking as it is here to protect our boundaries and us, I decide to let it leave my class with a scary image of it. They will not be so careless to get trapped in its light because of it. I therefore do not mention that was a joke as I swim back over to my class. Teacher leads the class back toward the city. A classmate asks, "How did you not get caught up in that fish's light Ann?"

I say, "Remember, I am a royal. The knowledge flood is immensely helpful. Also, teacher turned to face us. That is important changes near. His doing so made me take in more of my surroundings. I blinked to unfocused the light then I saw it. Plus, there are sketches in the castle library books of it and a little about what is known about it, including what we saw it do today."

My class shudders and thanks me for stopping them. I remind them it is my duty to protect them. The next day is the start of our three-day weekend. We have five days learning, three days off. I challenge them to a race around the city. All age three to age ten accept. There is only one older than ten that accepts. He is the son of one of my father's council. Twelve-year-old Meeke Mero.

CHAPTER THREE

Races

We race. I notice he stays five feet behind me and the rest stay behind him. They are all only pretending to do their best. It saddens me. I want to know how fast I am. How can I do that if they do not try to defeat me in a race? I challenged them. I want an actual race. The next two days are repeats of the race. Them deliberately failing. I figure I will have to race myself and my time to know if I get better. It sucks sometimes being a royal. I truly have no friends here. They will always remember I am their princess and next to rule. As if I ever asked to be born so. Life is a big adventure. I enjoy it I just wish for some actual friends that are not afraid to actually do their best against me. I hate their speed decreasing as they get close to me while we race. They try to put off they are tired. I know better.

I spend my school days learning as much as I can and my weekends timing myself and trying to beat my time. I get stronger and smarter. Then I learn shortcuts and increase my speed some more. After some years, another mer joins our races. This young female is three, a daughter of another council member. Meeke is eighteen now. I am nine and the rest that race me are between four and fourteen. They all still let me win. Boring. The next day instead of challenging them to race, I just swim pass them. I ditch them when they try to follow me.

CHAPTER FOUR

Exploring

They refuse to actually race then I will not ask any more or accept when they want to ask me to race. I swim to the boundaries and pass between two of the creepy fishes. I am far enough from both that neither see me. I feel alone here so far from every part of the city. I swim off at ease exploring the water around me. There is extraordinarily little light, plants, or animals here. It feels so empty. I swim up slightly to take in more of my surroundings. Nothing. I go higher. Still nothing. A bit higher. I see a small amount of light coming down from above. Still little to no plants or animals. I swim slowly to the light, being careful as I do not know what is there.

Every few tail flicks I move about two dozen feet higher. I pause at that time and look around. It is five rounds before I see plants, and a few sea animals. I recognize sharks and small clownfish. I also recognize some coral and seaweed. There are some plants I do not know and some animals I do not know. I go over to an animal with eight arms and touch it. I ask about what it is and its experiences. I am bombarded with images of things I do not know. I hear it be called an octopus. The plants are called kelp, and algae. I hear some of the other animals be called, sea dragons, viperfish, eels, whales, walrus, jellyfish, and squid.

Very overwhelmed, I go home. I am careful to enter from the exact location I left from. A few feet later I feel my parents' stress levels. I understand they are concerned about my disappearance. I go directly home. They asked where I went to. I reply, "Exploring the ocean. I am sorry I worried you."

CHAPTER FIVE

Guardian Encounters

The guardians show up. We face them quietly. One says, "Please relax. We will protect Ann, even as she explores. Learning about the ocean will teach her to better care for it and how to protect the people more. Be careful and stay safe Ann."

I reply, "I will. I have questions. What is kelp and algae?"

My parents look confused. A guardian says, "Some plants that grow higher than most mers swim. They stay where they are because they are content and happy. Why are you not happy?"

I look at the floor saying, "No friends. No one treats me as an equal. So, I go exploring and try to learn how to be the best ruler I can be for them one day. I also figure if I have not found anyone that I want by the time I am twenty, my parents or the guardians will end up choosing someone that could be trained to be a helper to me. Is that how my parents became my parents?"

Mom laughs, "Yes dear. I was chosen for your father. I fell in love with him about a year after we married. Months later, you were born. Now I have your father and you to love."

I ask, "Was there anyone else that you wanted before papa?"

Mom replies, "No. I knew nothing could ever be as my parents told me as long as I can remember that I was held to a stricter standard then they were because they had agreed with their king and queen that I was to be paired to their prince if he had not found anyone else by the time he was eighteen. We decided to leave you free to choose your own spouse."

I nod but mention again that no one treated me as an equal. Then I go to my room and get some rest. The next day, I again go out of the mer boundaries. I spend four hours outside of the boundaries before checking in. After lunch I again go out of the boundaries for another four hours. I meet almost all the creatures the octopus told me about and learn to tell the difference between kelp and algae. As the four-hour limit I placed on myself approaches I head home. I placed that limit on myself as that is the time I have after school and before dinner to myself. My parents have relaxed a tiny bit. After dinner I go to bed.

School the next day seems so long. I mean they talk about what I read about in-between my two outings yesterday. I have finished every book in our massive library. It has nothing about the creatures or plants I saw outside our boundaries. I readily opened the knowledge flow, so I learned more and there was truly little anyone knew that I had not read about. I do not ask but it is painful to be so trapped by their limited knowledge. After school, I rush off. In minutes, I have gone from the inner part of the city to our border that took my class two hours to reach the only time we ever came here. I pass through easily now. Then I swim up fast until I reach the place I was yesterday. Then I slow and learn as much as I can as I advance out and up.

CHAPTER SIX

Thinking Space and a Sea Dragon

My days and weeks repeat in this manner. A few months pass by. I come across a cave. I explore it. I run into the one creature the octopus told me about that I had not met before, a sea dragon. It spits a water ball at me. I catch it and toss it back. It swallows the water ball whole. We talk. I ask if I can visit its cave often. It agrees. One guardian shows up asking, "Enjoy my pet?"

I reply, "Your pet. That explains why it treats me so different than others do."

She laughs, "No. It treats everyone the same that is not a guardian. You react differently. Therefore, it respects you. It made this cave. You are safe here. It will not let anyone disturb you. You have questions your parents and people cannot answer. Do you not?"

I reply, "I do."

Then I ask my questions. Soon I learn as much as I can in the four hours. I go home and repeat that for a week. My questions have slowed. Time to explore more. I do that, going higher and out more. I meet seals, rays, crabs, clams, shrimp, oyster, urchins, and otters. I see sargassum, and mangrove.

CHAPTER SEVEN

Birthday Celebration

It takes me five months to process and learn about all of that. My tenth birthday is days away. School days. My birthday falls on the end of a normal school week, but my birthday is also a national holiday. Major dates in my life are entire national days off. My birth, age five (official school age), age ten (adult enough to choose a job if I was not royal born, yet as I am, it is the time I can officially join the council meetings if I want to. I think I am expected to, but I think I will swim unless made to join the meeting), my eighteenth birthday will be, as then I can get married. My twenty-first birthday will be if I have not taken overrule by then I will at that time. I do not agree with a national holiday as a child was born. I mean I am the same as most of them except I am in the royal family.

This year my classmates excitedly thank me for the holiday. As if I had a say in it. Yet for their excitement, I can not remove the law that I find stupid in celebrating as a national holiday the events of a royal's life. It is just a reason for the nation to take an extra day to relax and have some fun. Well that I cannot say I disagree with. They need time to relax also. I guess it was put into place to give the people some extra reasons to relax and have fun. I notice as the people get older, they tend to relax less, yet always find time to celebrate on national holidays. Leaving it there will help the adults have time off they might not get otherwise. So, I mention nothing about having found it stupid only hours ago.

My parents get me up early on my birthday, make me wear a nice dress, all in purple and gold tones. Then officially introduce me to their council. I do as expected and look at them directly until they drop their gaze. They officially recognize my right over them as they do so. It however tells me that even they will not be my friends first. I ask my parents if I can go swimming later. They tell me if I can wait until after everyone has given me gifts and not rush off as if I do not care about any of them I might. Annoying.

Yet I do as they ask. I be polite to all who give me a gift. That is at least every family in the nation. The wealthier families give me more gifts as they do individual gifts. I think they are trying to buy my favor. Little do they realize I despise having a holiday just because it is a birthday, so the more they give me, the less pleased I am. I actually favor the poorest family there. They got me a small card and a model of a mermaid that looks as me. It is probably the only friend I have. After all the gifts are given to me it is lunch time. After lunch, my parents tell everyone to enjoy their day off. I take that as my cue to leave and walk out. I walk until I reach the city limit then making sure I am alone I swim off as fast as I can.

Today I go even further then I had before. I meet seahorses, turtles, starfish, and dolphins. I see sea grass and sea lettuce. Learning about them helps me relax from the stupid holiday just because of my birthday. I think over the mer folk. Most of whom have the olive complexion, dark hair and either had green or blue eyes. Mer tails were scaled green and blue, with the exception of the healers and royal family. When we had legs and walking around our walkways a ribbon of our clan and family line and class was around our waist. So, everyone knew who they talked to if they need to. Healers have some shades of white in their tails and never touched a weapon. The royal family has shades of white and purple and could heal others but were also allowed to carry weapons. The royal family were the only ones that could heal and also touch weapons. Our appearances were affected by family line and the area of the kingdom we spent the most time in when we were not in school.

I know from the visiting Waters this morning that most magics are peaceful enough to not attack each other but not peaceful enough to marry outside of their magic for the most part and the exceedingly rare few that do marry their own energy type. Makes since. I do not inquire more. The Waters and Wateries that had visited greeted me politely then went over to my parents. The Wateries stopped a few feet closer but did not join the conversations. I realize they are the water nation's nobles, clan leaders and advisors to the ruler of the wateries. I briefly talk to them to introduce myself. They glance at my ribbon then address me as Princess Mer. That irritates me enough I soon found a reason to leave. No friends even among the water. I am lonely. I guess it will be this way until my parents or guardians choose someone for me. It really does not matter who is chosen as until I am married to whoever it ends up being, I am still the youngest unmarried royal of the mers. Even then I will be the mer ruler or heir still. Nothing will change as I still will not have a true friend.

Still thinking on the mers, time passes fast. Before to long a guardian touches my shoulder. As I look at her, she says, "It has almost been four hours young one. Do not stress your parents on your birthday. The people would feel it immensely today."

CHAPTER EIGHT

Loneliness and Boredom

I sigh and go home. The next day I tell my parents I was going to explore a few hours longer then normal. After a few minutes they nod, and I head out. I just go to my thinking place behind the water dragon and think some more on everything I have learned. Though there is more plants and animals away from the mer nation, I still have no friends. Am I to be this lonely for most or all my life? It seems extremely possible at this time.

After a while I decide to get some exercise and slowly swim through the water, doing laps. I have not done laps without racing others since I turned eight. I am so board. Yet the thought of going faster does not appeal to me either. There is nothing left to learn about and no one to race. Plus, I have no one to share with and no one can answer my questions except the guardians. I respect them a bit too much to ask questions without them prompting me to. The guardian that calls the water dragon a pet gave me a large amount of material today as a late birthday gift. She told me it would protect me from the elements and appear as what was right that I should wear in whatever color the viewer preferred. I have not a clue why she gave it to me and am afraid to have it on me. I left it in the cave.

After the time my parents allowed me nears an end, I go home. I know I will one day be responsible to care for all the Mers and protect them. If anything happened to me the people would panic as I have control of their protection field. That is the barrier that keeps outsiders from finding the kingdom. This barrier not only keeps us hidden it also provided air to the mers while we use our legs. Why do I have that control? Simple. I am the youngest royal. If I had any siblings, it would go to the strongest of us while the rest would cease to be royals after that one turned fourteen. It prevents overwhelming the people with the royal commands.

CHAPTER NINE

Exploring Further

Months pass by. I never touch the cloth I was given. I leave it in the cave and try not to spend much time there. I just lazily swim around at this level. As I pass a dolphin, I ask it to let me see a story, just to have something to do. I do not expect to be entertained. It tells me about a place that is dry with different plants and animals then I see here in the water. Oh, really? I have got to see this dry world for myself. I ask where it was.

Dolphin tells me up a bit, then to swim to the end of my sight lines. However, it warns me to avoid boats, that is things that float on the water. It tells me that the creatures on the boats kill all sorts of fish and my tail says I am a fish. It also mentions that they have things they call nets. The nets cut into flesh and trap many animals and would trap me also. It shows me all the images it saw so I know what to look out for. I thank the dolphin and its kinfolk for the information and help. Yet, my time is up today so learning more about the dry world has to wait. I go home.

After school the next day, I swim up some more from my hide out cave where the water dragon is. I feel thirstier here. With lower pressure around me I do not understand how that is. My body complains after a few minutes, so I rest at that point. Once adjusted I go a few minutes higher. Again, I have to rest because I am not use to the pressure differences. I only get up five dozen feet today before time nears an end. I usually get twenty dozen feet in that time. It takes me months to adjust to that enough to do the pressure adjustments as needed. Then I go further up.

Today I see a stranger, he looks somewhat similar to mers or wateries. I wonder what he is. I use my magic to say hi. When I get no response in the normal two minutes, I hide. The no response scares me. Yet I cannot help wondering about the way he swims. I mean he uses his legs! Does he not have a tail as mers do? Can he not be unseen as the wateries? Wait! Is he a part of the dry world? If he is then I am getting close. I cannot even ask him because he does not understand me.

How does he swim that way? I focus on my city looks and make the change to have my legs. PAIN! I feel as if I am being stabbed all through my legs and lungs. I quickly drop that and go back to my hideout cave. I rest there the rest of my time before I go home. No point of entering the mer boundaries in pain. That would stress my parents and all the people. Nearly a year passes by before I can swim as that stranger male did. I am clumsy about it. I turn eleven tomorrow.

After my small party, which is to say, it is not as many gathering as a national holiday I go for a swim. I come across some wateries. I say hi and introduce myself. Though I do not mention being a royal they know it because my tail is purple. They say, "Why would a mer royal want to visit with us Merth Ann?"

Sighing I reply, "Just being friendly."

I leave soon after as I know they will not drop my royal rank. Their calling me by my full name is enough proof of that when I only said my name was Ann. I go to the area I saw the stranger male in and try again to swim as he did. I try to get faster. I have a tiny speed increase. Not good enough. Out of time. I judge my speed by how many laps I can do in my allowed time. I have marked two spaces and swim laps between those points. With my tail I can do that distance three hundred times in four hours. I barely get to twenty times with my legs now.

Days later, I see that stranger male again. I stay as far from him as I can. I notice he does not go deeper than the lightest area of the water, where I can see for thousands of miles. The lowest he goes is a hundred feet from where the water changes to air. This the animals have told me is called the ocean's surface. So, if he gets too close to me, I will swim down hard. Besides, I know I can outswim most. Only because I am not using my tail where this stranger comes does he get even as close to me as fifty feet away. He tries to get closer, but I maintain that distance. As time I have nears an end, I hide from him while he has his back to me. A few minutes later he gives up looking for me and I am able to swim home safely.

It takes me to nearly my twelfth birthday before I can swim with my legs as fast as I can with my tail. I am now nearly sure most do not stand a chance in races against me. Of course, they might if they actually tried. I do not challenge the wateries, as I would have to force them to stay seen so I could know where they were, which is unfair to them. My parents are too busy to race me. My people do not try to beat me though they agree to race. Most of the time I think they take my question as a command. It has long sense ceased to be fun. I cannot even communicate with the stranger so I cannot race him. I am now firmly convinced he is part of the dry world. I mean the way he swims, how long and how deep he swims is statement enough of that. Plus, I noticed as he gets tired, he heads up.

Today I reach the area as he is getting tired. I stay hidden and follow where he goes. I get to a place the animals tell me is called a shore. They do not know what is pass the shore. There are different types. They have shown me that some are rocky, some partly rocky and some are as this one I have arrived at, gritty. The animals have told me this gritty stuff under my feet is called sand. Off a bit I see some of what they call trees. I walk around on the sand for an hour before my time is up. I scrub my feet hard that night, just trying to remove the feeling of grit from them.

As usual my father had said good night to me before I entered my room. Also, as usual mom waited until after my bath. A bath for a sea creature might seem strange to you folks of the dry world. It is more as moving through and over sea urchins. They remove foreign particles from our skin. It feels wonderful actually. Mom notices my bath was longer than usual. She asks about that. I say, "I explored an area with more grit then we have here in the nation. I wanted the grit off of my body."

Mom says, "Alright. Be careful while exploring Ann. We love you."

I nod, hug her and tell her I love her too. Soon we say our goodnights and she leave. The next day I go to the shore again after school. I walk along it for a bit then turn and walk back. I do not dare go too far before knowing the movements made in this dry world.

CHAPTER TEN

Water Help

Water princess Wela comes over to me. She asks, "Lost Ann?"

I reply, "No. I do not know how those that live here act. I do not want them to wonder about me."

Wela says, "You are quite far from home."

I ask, "Point?"

Wela asks, "Do your parents know you left?"

I say, "They know I explore beyond the nation's boundaries."

Wela asks, "Do they know you are surface side? Do they know you swim as a dry world person?"

I say, "How does that concern you?"

Wela says, "It does not. I just think I can help you learn the movements the dry people make by helping you stay hidden while we watch them. I just do not want your parents mad with me."

I say, "We are just playing together. Are we not?"

She laughs, "Sure, playing. Hide and go see. A variation of hide-n-seek."

We laugh. I do as she suggests and go back into the water. She wraps her arm around my waist then we are miles down the shore. Wow the water can move fast. There I see a couple walking along the shore. Their movements are similar to my parents. When his hand moves down from her waistline Wela moves us miles down shore. I ask about that. Wela says, "Watched that once. No desire to see it again. She is not his first. He might be her first though."

I say, "I do not understand."

Wela says, "Well, the dry world people, at least some, do not seem to be mated once as we are."

I say, "Enough info on that."

Wela says, "I thought so. I doubt you wanted to see it."

I agree that I do not want to see a couple's personal time. We watch the dry world people until I have to head home. This continues for a month. Then I am comfortable enough with their movements to act as one of them. I have heard some of the language but I do not know the meanings so I still cannot communicate with them. I go sit in my thinking space; the cave guarded by the water dragon. Its owner the guardian shows up. I stand saluting. She laughs, "Relax Ann."

CHAPTER ELEVEN

Friend

D oing so I say, "Miss guardian."
She says, "My name is Meme. I see you are mimicking the dry people."

I wonder, "Am I wrong to?"

Meme replies, "No child. It is best you do so when near them. It will keep you safer. Just as swimming the way they do keeps you safer near them."

I say, "Well the animals mentioned they kill fish and my tail says I am a fish."

Meme laughs, "Good creatures that tell you things to make you consider how to stay the safest. Any questions?"

I ask, "Why do you let me know your name?"

Meme replies, "Not just know it Ann. When a guardian rank tells you their name, they are giving you permission to use it. However, unless you are told directly the permission does not exist."

I say, "So, why do you allow me to use your name Meme?"

Meme says, "You are so similar to me. I did not have many friends growing up. I thought you might want a friend."

I hug her weeping. She is the first friend I have. Wela was after something, I am sure. I just do not know yet what. Meme hugs me until I calm down. Then she says, "Get some rest Ann. I will let your parents know you are with me. Learning. They have no need to know what you are learning. It would only scare them."

Happy yet scared I get some sleep. When I wake up Meme says, "I told your parents you would be with me for a week. That should give you some time to learn about the dry people. Just be careful to stay hydrated enough."

Excited I hug her. She swims me toward the surface. As we near the dry people's limit, I as normal change my looks to that. Meme lets go of me. I swim the rest of the way alone. She was much faster than I am. About half my time. Since she knows I go surface side and has gotten me a week off of reporting home every night, I decide to see how much I can learn today.

I listen to as much of the dry people's conversations as I can before I feel very thirsty. I go for a swim. The dry people do not seem to need as much water as I do. Still they can not drink sea water at all or get hydrated as I can. My gills, hidden as they are, allow me to intake water easily when I am in the water. I need water more then air.

Rounds this way. When I think I am getting sentence structure down I go to my thinking space. There I practice the sentences I have heard. Meme tells me the meaning as she had a watery guardian help her learn them so she could help me. The wateries can go more inland, onto the dry world then I can as there is also rivers, lakes and ponds they can move into. That allows them to learn the dry people's languages better. Plus, they have had generations of hearing it, so they are good with the meanings now. After I know the meanings Meme and I talk in that language. I ask, "Meme, why are you talking to me in the dry people's language?"

Meme replies, "Your being able to communicate the way they do will keep you safer near them. I help you learn whatever will keep you safe."

I thank her. Our week passes this way. The evening I have to go home Meme and some of her equals wait for me in the cave. I am startled to see them all. Meme says, "Relax Ann. We are here to help you if you ever need us."

Another says, "Princess Ann, you need to be careful. These outsiders you take the appearance of might harm you. If they found out you are a mermaid, your life could be in danger. They are not magic and fear those who have magic, and some of them hurt those they fear. The name Merth is an indicator of your magic. Do not use it in their presence."

The rest of them nod. Realizing they want me safe, I reply, "Honored guardians, I will be careful. Might I please have permission to explore their dry world? I want to learn about the plants and animals there. I want to know why our sea is so good to us, and how to better take care of my home and people. Please let me learn."

Meme says, "We allow you to. Only stay close to the water for easy access home. If you are touching the water, we will know that you are safe or not. If you are not safe, we can help you as long as you are in the water. We just want you to come home safe. OK. Learning about the dry world will teach you why you love the sea and its life better. It will make you more able to make wise decisions for the mers."

I say, "Thank you. I agree to do my best to come home safe."

Meme says, "Good. Ann, please continue with your four-hour time frames you had before this past week. It will keep you from dehydrating. Also, the longer you are away from the mer nation the more the mers worry."

Nodding I promise, "I will be careful my friends, my protectors."

They truly are the only friends I currently have. Wela wanted fish for her people. As a royal of the fish folk, I can give her that. Though her people can do without us mers we cannot deal without her people cleaning our waters. So, I would have even if she just asked. I am glad she has enough thoughtfulness to at least offer something in exchange. I go home as the time Meme had gotten me is over.

CHAPTER TWELVE

Council Meeting

The next day I turn fourteen. My parents tell me that as guardian saw fit to personally train me, I most certainly was ready to join the council meetings. Therefore, I was expected to attend today's council meeting. There goes swimming and dry world exploring today. Bummer. Still, I know I will one day have to do these on my own as ruler so learning how they are done will help. It seems that it will be sooner than when I turn twenty-one thanks to my week away. Unexpected consequences.

After lunch, is the council meeting. My father sits on the throne. Mom sits beside him. The throne is just wide enough for the two of them. I chose to sit at their feet asking to just observe. When it is only my family and the council in the room, I notice a seal go around the room preventing anyone outside the room from hearing. That explains why I never could tell what the meetings were about even with my knowledge flow open receiving. Warrior asks, "What did guardian teach you Ann?"

I say, "Many things. I am sure all of what I learn will help me make good decisions for the mers one day."

Father says, "Alright meeting. What has happened in the pass month?"

All seven of them talk at once. Everything is the usual. Well I knew that even without this meeting. Why are monthly meetings necessary? Mom glances at me then asks, "Got anything to add Ann?"

I state, "I just want to observe today."

It remains silent. After a few minutes, my father says, "You say that Ann, yet your eyes say you have questions."

I sigh, "Why monthly meetings?"

Father says, "It gives me a chance to visit with my friends mainly. We get the business out of the way first. Also, in these meetings we can plan for events for the people. Such as the national holidays. Your wedding one day will be."

I say, "Until I saw how excited the people were for such events on my tenth birthday, I did not understand them. I had thought about removing them until I saw their excitement. Then I realized some adults do not truly relax without a holiday. Therefore, giving them a reason to do so is good."

Healer says, "It also lowers their stress so improves their health. That makes things easier for my clan."

Food producer says, "It helps my clan clear off some of the dying coral and seaweed, so we maintain a healthier food supply easier."

Our food gatherer says, "That makes it easier to know what we pick will be good for the people even if it is older growth."

Sea life helper says, "The healthier we are, the better we can help the sea life maintain their health. The animals in return help us if we need it, give us color and entertainment. The only ones that do not are the creepy border fish. They help us protect our boundaries though."

Repairer mentions, "Easier to repair things if we are healthy and relaxed."

Builder says, "Easier to build new homes or art if we are not getting sick or tired and stressed."

At that I inject, "Most of us only have one child. Would that not nearly half our numbers every generation?"

Mom says, "I use to think that. It is balanced out by others joining the mers and never going back to wherever they lived before, the few second children we have, and guardians helping our population numbers if we dip low."

I nod. Warrior says, "The national holidays help my clan keep our alertness. You test our limits often. Where do you disappear from and to?"

His clan I do not understand the need for, so I just reply, "Find out on your own."

I understand healers to heal, the clan that grew the food, the clan that gathered the plants for the food and medicines, the clan that helped the sea life. Those that repaired the nation, the builders that added to the boundaries I do understand; but why did we have a need for a warrior clan? It does not matter. I will know when I rule in less then seven years at the rate of them making me join this meeting today.

Soon after the meeting ends. Noticing this is about the time school usually ends I ask, "Mom, dad, might I go exploring?"

They laugh that some things never change and allow me to. Knowing the warriors will try to find where I leave from, I make sure I get out of there fast. I use my knowledge flow to make sure I avoid them all. I race to the surface making the adjustments as needed and ten minutes later, change into my legs. It has gotten less painful to do so but still hurts some.

CHAPTER THIRTEEN

Meeting Dry People

I swim directly to shore. I see a creature the sea life has told me is a seagull, a type of bird about a dozen feet away. I walk toward it, calling out with my magic that I want to know what it has experienced. It moves into the air as I get close. I do not think it wants to share with me. I try starfish. They share that the dry animals do not trust the dry people and as I appear as one, they do not trust me. I know I cannot look as part of the sea near where dry people visit so I have no choice except to let it go. Animals not responding to me in kindness is not something I am used to.

Oh well. I walk the shore. Soon I come across two people yelling at each other. I understand that from their gestures before even hearing the words. He hits her. I am stunned. No mer male ever hit the mer females. They took good care of us. That does not include the training courses. In those everyone was considered genderless. Still once done with training the males would take the front of the pain so us females had an easier time. I have never witnessed a male give pain to a female. He scares me. Yet trained as a warrior I cannot ignore someone in need. I grab a piece of tree and run to place myself between them. I face the man threatening him with the tree piece I later learn is called a stick. He swings his fist at me.

Well some use for the warrior training I was required to take. I dodge and swing my feet, flipping him onto his back while I landed on my feet again. I might not know why a warrior clan yet but am I sure glad for the training they put me through. He tries to kick me. I jump and land on his ankle. He screams as I hear a bone crack. I get off his ankle, help the woman up and we walk away from him.

As we walk, well more precisely I walk and she somewhat drags one foot she says, "Thank you. How did you learn that? Would you teach me? Please slow down. I am in pain."

At that healer training takes over. I cannot let her suffer. I do not know if I am strong enough to carry her, but I am not doing medicine near the male. Not giving him a chance to sneak up on us. I lift her into my arms and slowly move forward. She stares at me. My eyes I am sure are solid black from the effort I am putting out to keep her from getting injured more. Once we reach the tree line, I notice a river. It flows directly to the ocean. Good, I am now thirsty. I set her down. Then I submerge my face into the water. Much better. I hear Meme ask, "Why are you so tired already Ann?"

I whisper what happened. Meme says, "Outsiders cannot handle our medicines child. At least Water, my equal says so."

Swell. I have no idea what to do for the woman now and as a healer I can not leave her alone without help. Raising from the water, I say, "I am Ann."

She replies, "Martha. How did you learn that?"

I ask, "Learn what?"

Martha says, "Breaking his ankle. I have wanted to for years. That way I could escape his beating me."

I say, "Well you do not need it now. I only attacked as I saw him hit you. No male should hit a female. How are you in pain?"

Martha says, "My ankle is twisted badly. I have other pain, but I am not sure what is wrong. Could you get me to a doctor?"

I say, "I do not know what you mean by doctor."

Martha looks at me curiously. I realize I said something she found strange. I say, "My parents did not get out much and neither did I.

Their friends trained me so no stranger could hurt me."

She says, "Surely you had someone to look after your health needs."

I say, "A healer. Well then I will carry you to the nearest healer you know."

Martha directs me to the nearest doctor she knows of. We go inland. Thankfully, we stay near enough to the river I can see it. I avoid the houses until Martha points to one saying, "Doctor Madeline lives there."

I say, "Fine. I need to set you down anyways."

Placing her down I put my arm around her waist and walk to the house. She does her best to keep by my side but I have to go slow so she can keep up. I am almost out of time and have not explored as much as I would have wanted. Darn healer codes! Oh well, I cannot ignore her need even if it puts me late getting home. We reach the door and she knock. Moments later, an elder woman opens the door. I say, "Martha says you know medicines. She needs help."

The woman says, "Martha needs medical help now. She needs to get away from her husband permanently, so this does not happen again. I told you Martha, he has not changed. You cannot go back."

Martha says, "I know. I thought he was going to kill me today. I just have nowhere else to go."

At the realization that it is her husband that treated her so, I dry heave, collapsing onto my knees. I move away as the doctor moves close to me asking what is wrong. I gasp out, "Take care of Martha. She is needing you. I just have never come across any male that would hurt a female, let alone their spouse before. I will be fine."

She asks, "You sure?"

I nod. She moves back to Martha. I down my emotional health mix as neither could see me to do so. I have no intentions of sharing mer medicines with strangers. Then I go over to them completely fine. I ask, "What all is paining Martha?"

Doctor Madeline replies, "Lots of bruises, some minor cuts, a twisted ankle, and a broken rib cage. It will be months before she heals. Sadly, she should not move in that time and her husband will look for her. This is one of the first places he will look as I care for the injured. No one will say that she was not seen coming this direction, not when he threatens them or their families. I can not even try to stop him from forcing her to go back with him as many people need my help. I cannot help others if I get beaten so bad, I cannot move. I fear for Martha's life if he should find her."

I ask, "Martha, are you wanting to leave him?"

Martha replies, "Yes."

I ask, "At what cost?"

Martha says, "The only things I have left are my life and what I wear."

I ask, "Would you risk your life to get away from him?"

Martha replies, "Madeline is right, I will die if I stay. Do you know a place I can run to and be safe?"

As I smile, Martha asks, "Where?"

I reply, "To my home. That is provided you can make it there. You could get help getting there but those who could help might not trust you."

Martha asks, "How would I get their trust?"

I ask, "Have you ever lied to anyone?"

Martha replies, "Not that I remember. Then again, I am not sure as I have been beaten so mush some of my memories are incomplete. I do not know if I remember everything."

I ask, "To your knowledge, have you ever killed someone?"

Martha replies, "No."

I ask, "Have you ever intentionally hurt someone without doing so to protect life?"

Martha replies, "Not in my memories."

I say, "When you need to run, do so. Run to the ocean or a river that flows to it. Ask to go to my home. Drop this into the water. You will be taken to my home."

Then I hand her one of my tail scales. Martha says, "It feels as a fish scale, but it is purple. I have never seen a purple fish before."

I say, "It is hard to come across. Only three people can pass it to anyone else. It could only be turned over to one of those three people. They are my parents and me. My father will not ask for it. My mother might demand it. Ask to live in their home before you release it, as only they can see if you could. That scale will get you help getting there. It is an honor code not shared with many. I expect punishment for my giving it to you."

Martha says, "I cannot accept it if you will get punished for it."

I grin, "What do I have to fear about being told to stay in the city they live in for a month. Saving your life would be worth it. Of course, I hope not to be disciplined. Keep the scale. You might need it."

Martha says, "Thank you then."

As she puts it into a pocket her husband comes in. I move between them. He draws a knife. I ask, "Want a round two?"

He lunges at me. I dodge and again knock him off his feet. He says something I have not learned the meaning of. I do not care for his tone. I later learned he had cussed at me. His tone caused me to kick him. I am a princess! No one talks to me in that tone, except my parents and the guardians. He grabs my ankle as I kick him again for insulting me. He had called me an ugly dog. I twist my foot and we hear bones break. I press slightly causing him to scream. I say, "Martha is no longer yours. You broke the protection right clause."

When he jabs his blade into the back of my leg, I put full pressure on his wrist completely breaking it. As he tries to move his hand, I step off of his wrist then down my physical realignment mix, followed by the skin and muscle healing mix. In seconds, I feel as if

I had not received any wounds. I feel it and sure enough, I am not hurt anymore. I say, "I hope that hurt. All the time I hated defense training, yet here I am using it. Are you after a round three? I could break your other ankle and wrist for you."

I see the doctor trying awfully hard not to laugh. She is incredibly pleased with his pain. Not suited, but I cannot say I blame her if she has healed Martha so much to know without being told he was the cause of Martha's pain. I say, "I thought you were a healer. You have no business being so happy about his pain."

Doctor Madeline says, "He does not matter to me. Every time Martha has been healed enough to leave; she ends up back here, desperately fighting to live within two days. You have not even caused him one-one hundredth of the pain he has caused her. I find it good to see him on the receiving end of pain for once."

I ask, "True Martha?"

Martha replies, "I have been here so often I might find my way in the dark."

My anger and defensiveness soars at her words and I deliver a kick into her husband's side. That breaks his elbow and rib cage. Much too satisfying to see him drop in pain. The doctor whispers, "The first time I saw Martha she had been raped. Her parents made her get married claiming she would never be desired by anyone else. They have been together since. Most of that time she was in a bed under my care, trying to save her life."

I ask, "Who did that to her?"

CHAPTER FOURTEEN

Red Water

No response is voiced. I glance at Martha and she is looking at the floor. I glance at the doctor and she is looking at the male with disgust and distrust. Then the realization that her parents forced her to marry one who hurt her sets in. I master red water in seconds. I know I do as I tossed a ball of it at him. One ball, two, three. I soon lose count. Dizzy. So dizzy. I make sure he passes out before I stop. I am very dehydrated. I face the doctor saying, "I know I do not have to ask, I will anyways. Please let him suffer."

Doctor Madeline replies, "As perverted as it may be for a doctor to say so, I say 'With extreme pleasure.'"

I say, "Martha, come with me. I will directly take you to the city I live in. He will never hurt you again. Madam Madeline, I would appreciate it if no one knows I was here. It would not go over well."

She nods. I help Martha outside. I am now at my thirty-minute warning to get home. I am not going to make it. However, I can send a message I will be a bit late if Wela will help me. My parents will understand once I explain things to them. I help Martha to the ocean's edge. There I call out, "Wela, did you see what occurred earlier?"

Wela walks over to us from off a bit replying as she gets close, "Sure did. Why do you ask?"

I reply, "I have to take her to the city to save her life. Thing is I can not get her there safely and get home on time. Please tell my parents that I am running late, on my way home but am slower than normal and will explain when I arrive."

Wela says, "I might. You owe me."

I say, "Sure. Thank you."

Wela dives. Soon she gets to low for us to see her. I ask, "Can you swim?"

Martha says, "No."

I say, "This will be scary then. Hold the scale I handed you to your face. I will help you get to the city."

With that we walk into the water. Martha whines slightly from pain as we move. I must get her away from the bad male. I make her continue. Once I feel the ledge drop off signaling the deeper waters, I say, "Martha, place the scale over your face now and hold it there. Just trust me."

Though scared, Martha does as I told her. I instantly propel us down a hundred feet before changing to having my tail while I let her adjust to the pressure differences. I take her down as fast as she can handle it. I know with her using my scale, I could tire out faster. When I near my thinking space I notice Martha is losing consciousness. So not good. We are only about halfway there. I call out, "Meme, help!"

She is by me in moments. Meme wonders, "Why bring an outsider this far child? She is hurting also. It is surprising she is still alive with how injured she is. Do you not have sense?"

I say, "Her parents forced her to be with one who had hurt her. I saw him beating her. I could not leave her there. She is losing consciousness. I cannot take her back to that situation, and at current, we cannot go further. I also attacked the one hurting her more then once. He now has a broken ankle, wrist, and rib. Plus, I think I water burned him. I know I mastered red water. Hearing her parents made her be with him made me irritated enough that I was throwing red water balls at him before I even thought of it. Is it wrong I asked the healer for the dry people not to help him?"

Meme leads me into my thinking space. Then says, "Tark, dry the cave."

Her sea dragon turns yellow. The cave is dry in seconds. My tail vanishes as my legs appear. Meme sits by Martha and me as we wait for Martha to wake back up.

Meme says, "It was wrong of you to put a healer in the position of choosing between helping someone and obeying you."

I say, "She was not going to help him anyways. She told me how much he hurt Martha. She mentioned Martha was back to her place in need of help within two days of being well enough to leave every time for years. She had no desire to help him. Not even her healer training could stop her from hiding her pleasure at my hurting him. He really deserves the pain. Such a person is a scorn to all life."

Meme laughs. Then mentions I should have at least reminded a healer of the health codes. However, it was done, and she did not know if she would have done any better.

Hours later, Martha groans, "Where are we?"

I say, "Halfway to my home."

Martha asks, "We swam here?"

I reply, "Yes. We still have to swim also. Let me know when you feel up to that. Guardian, are my parents worried?"

Meme replies, "I told them you were with me and would be for a bit. We were helping someone heal. Why do you not use my name?"

I say, "Martha might without your permission. She is in enough pain without punishment for something she does not understand."

Meme looks at Tark then says, "My pet is tiring. The cave will be filled with water in five minutes."

I say, "Well Martha, you have five minutes before we continue to my home."

Martha asks, "What is---?"

I cut her off saying, "Do not speak any name unless one tells you their name personally. Safer that way. That is what she calls her pet. It is a sea dragon. The first time I entered this cave, it blasted me with a water ball. I react faster then most so it lets me come here. That plus guardian is my friend."

Meme says, "Tark cannot see if she is able to come here on her own because of how hurt she is."

I say, "If she had remained conscious, I could set her ankle now. As it is, we have to wait."

Five minutes later, I say, "Martha, hold the scale over your face again. We are about to swim."

Martha obeys. Tark releases the hold on the water. As it hits me my legs change into my tail. Meme grabs Martha's other side. She uses magic to tell me we got to get down fast. We dive three hundred feet before I feel Martha is experiencing pressure differences. Meme feels it to. We stop. Meme tells me to ask for the wateries to adjust the pressure between here and my home. I do so. One minute later, we go down again. This time there is no breaks to let Martha adjust. There is no need. I will remember the wateries can control water pressure as well.

An hour later, we enter the mer boundaries. In minutes, we approach the city. Meme leaves. I swim Martha to the walkway closest to me then we walk toward the castle. I say, "Walk paths have the air you are used to friend. We check in first. Then you see a healer. This is home."

Two minutes later, we come across the warrior clan leader. He is expressive about his displeasure of an outsider being here. I say, "What outsider? This is my distant cousin. Her name is Martha. Excuse us, my parents must be worried about me and she needs healer help immediately. Have healer come to the castle, now."

It takes him a moment as I walk on with Martha to reply, "Yes Princess."

I try to ignore that. Martha asks, "Princess?"

Sighing I reply, "I am. You noticed he did not bow. No one here does. It would be rejected if they did. I will not own slaves. Neither would my parents. The gesture he did on seeing me is the highest form of respect here. Everyone that deserves respect gets saluted. It is different on how many get the respect for different people. Royals get everyone's respect. Guardians get more. That is why they are not seen much. Do not mention meeting her. That is something special. I do not know if you would have met her had I not needed help getting you here. Give me my scale. You will not need it anymore as you are not able to leave the city on your own unless you become one of us."

Martha says, "Nothing left for me in that place we left from. Why are we in the sea?"

I say, "The sea is home. I am a mermaiden. The male we came across is a merman. Everyone here is a mer except you. Some are leery of you because you are not one of us, but that is not something you are at fault for. I think that it comes from your people's boats killing fish and hurting other sea life in the thousands. I really want to know about your home. I could see your memories if you let me, but it is too much for you right now. What was the first thing that male called me? I did not understand fully his words, only his tone. I kicked him as he had no right to use that tone with me."

Martha replies, "It was an insult. Not a good term. I do not want to talk about him."

I nod. We reach the castle entrance. The guards look at Martha full of questions, but they do not ask as it is for my parents to decide. I lead Martha into the throne room. My father questions, "Why bring an outsider to our city Ann?"

CHAPTER FIFTEEN

New Mers

Knowing this is a touchy issue for many people, I reply, "Papa, the healer codes say we never leave alone one who needs medical help. I could not ignore her need. The closest healer of her kind was not able to help her. She has suffered for years there. The healer saving her life many times only for her to be fighting to live within a couple days as the one she was trapped with would hurt her. At this moment, she has bruises, cuts, a twisted ankle and a broken rib. I could not leave her there to go through everything again."

Mom says, "Understandable. Still, why not take her to another city she is used to?"

I reply, "Mom, her tormentor could find her there. She cannot swim so he would not even think that she would go to the sea without their crafts. She is here now. She could easily stay on our walkways and live safely. Or she could become one of us and move more freely. Either way, she lives a lot more peacefully then she has in years."

Mom says, "Show me what you saw that you would risk your safety for Ann."

I sit Martha into a chair so she can rest then walk over to my mom. I focus on what I had come upon and the conversation and actions in the house. I do not think of the outside locations. In moments of my mom making the link to me she closes it turning to papa crying. Mom says, "Marco."

It was a whine. I never knew my mom whined so. My father wraps her in a hug. Mom says, "We cannot send her back Marco. Not even if she had not seen this place could we send her back. We cannot. It would be wrong. Let her be one of us so she can live on our foods. Please Marco. Please."

As she breaks down into tears papa touches their foreheads together. Minutes later, He says, "Martha can join the mers. First though the four of us need healing. Come."

I help Martha up. We follow my parents. Papa is keeping the people from noticing mom's tears. We enter the healing area. We go to the highest level in moments. In moments, my parents are well as they only needed the emotional mix. I refuse to take it. I already treated myself above the sea, so I know I have adjusted much. They do not know I already had some and press the issue. I just tell them, "Only way I get better than I am is to take the memory mix. I need to remember. It will give me a bases to help the people one day, so I can make sure we do not go that way."

Healer says, "Well then Ann, what is Martha needing healed from?"

I say, "Bruises, cuts, twisted ankle, and a broken rib currently. I was told she has suffered many years barely living many times. I do not know if her older wounds ever healed properly. I doubt it. How many broken bones have you suffered over the years Martha?"

Martha replies, "In the past five years alone, nearly every part of my body has been broken at one point or another. I am nearly sure only my skull has not been broken because that would be attempted murder and the king of the nation where I had lived would be informed of that as it is law."

Mom asks, "Yet a person can beat another until death nearly occurs yet get away with it?"

Martha says, "He claims it was an accident. Those who know better are to afraid of him for themselves or their families to say differently. The king stopped listening to reports about him being severely abusive. I was unable to even talk the few times I was allowed to meet alone with the king. Most of the time the one who hurt me was there and I was too afraid to talk. The royal family is kind. They do not allow such things. Those who knew what was occurring to save their own lives or their families lives were made to make the king and his family believe I was very clumsy. If Ann had not saw it for herself, she might not have believed me."

I scuff, "What kind of person do you take me for Martha? I would realize that no one even clumsy could hurt themselves the amount you are hurt."

Martha says, "No one gets to see me until I am mostly healed."

Healer questions, "What about your parents? Did they believe you were clumsy?"

Martha slurs, "Who cares? They do not care about me."

Healer says, "Surely they do."

She would assume such. I would have too, if I had not been told how they forced her into that situation. I say, "Do not use our ways to judge her past Janice. Martha was violated. Her parents then made her marry him. She is nothing to them. She has lived since in that pain. It is why I had to bring her here, so she could finally heal and actually live. Maybe she can learn to be happy."

Janice is pale as she says, "You did not seriously accuse her parents of that."

I say, "I did. I saw the truth in her eyes when I expect the closest thing, she had to an ally there told me. I had trouble accepting it. I wanted to be sick but the one who hurt her had found us. I was instantly shifted into warrior mode to protect myself, Martha and her ally. I hurt him bad, cannot say I have any symphony for him and brought Martha here as fast as I safely could."

Janice says, "They could not be her birth parents then. No one treats their child that way. Plus, she did not get married willingly which is void of the document. Martha is an older child lost at sea. In a year I am sure she will know our ways well and can then choose a job. Maybe one day find love. Here Martha, drink this. It heals old wounds first. Painful though."

Martha states, "I doubt much could be more painful then what I went through."

She drinks it. In moments, Martha is crying. Ten minutes later, Martha goes to sleep. Janice says, "We wait until she wakes up. Warrior had someone tell me you wanted me at the castle immediately. I assume Martha was the reason. I would have come there, except you got here first. I was helping someone have their babies. A rare set of twins. They are in the next room."

I say, "Twins? Let us see them."

Mom says, "Yes, twins is rare."

Dad says, "Alright then."

Janice shows us to the next room. We stay back as Janice asks the woman how she feels and checks her vitals. Then she checks on the twins. As she checks the second one, she sighs, "Low vitals."

I am by Janice in a moment and take hold of the little girl. I ask, "What is her name?"

The baby's mother replies, "Princess, I have not named my babies yet. I have not got over the shock of having twins."

I carry her over to her mother and place the baby on the woman. In that moment, the little one's vitals even out. They are study and good now. Janice asks, "Why did you do that? How did you know it would help?"

Pleased it worked, I reply, "Read it somewhere while exploring. Did not know it works but it was worth the risk. I mean Sea-tone could not get much worse. So, there was a greater chance of her recovering."

Dad says, "Ann! You should not name other's children for them."

Mom says, "Why would you do that Ann?"

I say, "Sorry. I had not realized I did. I was just thinking of the tones the sea makes as I listened to her heartbeat. It sounds similar. So similar. Waves against rocks, waves against the gritty surfaces, waves through the coral."

When I wake up, I am on a bed by Martha. Meme says, "I told you she was only tired. She did not sleep while Martha was under her care. Two full days. I think she might have lasted a bit longer if she had not named a baby."

I say, "I knew I was getting tired. How is little Sea-tone now?"

Meme says, "Much improved. She eats as her twin does now. She will live."

I say, "That was what I was after, both living."

Meme says, "You succeeded. However, your naming the child makes her stronger than others. Such as she could unintentionally become a clan leader. Never accept her not giving her best. You will know if she is not as her heartbeat will flux into its birth pattern if she is trying hard. That will cause her to slow lots and breathe hard. For a while let her teachers and same age learn as you had wanted to. She will not be as lonely as you were if she is allowed to learn that way."

I say, "No one treats me as an equal. I have very few friends."

Martha says, "I consider you a friend."

I say, "Martha, you respect me for my fighting skills that got you away from that place while you were alive. Yet you still called me princess when you heard another do so. That will always be on your mind in decisions you make. I have little true friends."

Papa says, "Better then the no friends you claimed a year ago."

I say, "I have the best friends a mer could ask for. The guardians. Still I feel respect and do not ask questions unless they prompt me to. I do not race them. There are none that treat me as an equal that I also treat as equals. I am alone. I do figure you and mommy will one day end up choosing my spouse for me. Please make sure he is nothing as Martha was trapped by for years. I cannot live that way."

A few days later, the twins are old enough to be introduced to everyone and Martha is mostly healed. Papa has told everyone today is a national holiday. Everyone wonders what event we are celebrating. As everyone gathers in the great room where the throne is, Papa says, "Today is a celebration of us gaining three new mers. Mersa, please introduce your twins to everyone."

Mersa says, "Thank you sire. As our king mentioned, I had twins a few days ago. Their names are Sea-tones and Water-waves Mersome. Both girls. I ask no more than four visitors at a time. Thank you."

She sits back down. Papa then says, "Our other new national is Martha Merson. She is an older child lost at sea. We cannot send her back. While she is past age to choose her job, we think it is best if she learns a bit about each clan first to see what she prefers. Martha had a rough time surface side. Enough that she is currently under healer care, so take it easy on her alright."

The people mutter an agreement. Martha stands up as papa tells her to introduce herself. She says, "As sire mentioned, I am Martha. I had an extremely hard surface life. I prefer not to talk about it at this time as I am still recovering from the wounds it left me with. Just know Ann saved my life. Sire I want to learn warrior skills, for a warrior saved me."

At that a gasp goes around. Mummers start, "What does she mean a warrior saved her? How could a warrior save a person drowning? Perhaps she is mistaken?"

I stand up. Instant silence. I say, "Martha is not mistaken. I was in warrior mode when we met. Someone was attacking her. It is just the way that person is. An outsider. I defended her, then kept her from drowning as I brought her here. Now she is one of us. You know as a royal I know both healing and fighting. She met me as a warrior first, so she is right, a warrior saved her."

Someone asks, "What did you come across to be a warrior first?"

Papa says, "No one can handle that information. At least until Martha can share it."

CHAPTER SIXTEEN

Council United to See What I Saved Another From

The council stands. Instant quiet from everyone. Janice says, "If we are facing a mass pain event, the council needs to be prepared. I need to know so I can help others recover."

Papa says, "Agreed. Ann show the council what you came across."

I say, "Mom could not handle it. There is no way they could."

Janice says, "I know we cannot. Still we need to know."

I focus on parts of my memory. Then on the council. I show them my seeing a small island above me. The next image they get is the male hitting Martha. My fight with the male. My picking Martha up. Then I jump images to being inside the doctor's home and the information she gave me. My second fight with the male. The knowledge that Martha's parents had put her into that situation. Then the swim home. Martha passing out. Guardian and I reviving her. Ending with getting her here. I had kept them from seeing most of the scenery. I only allowed them to know the meanings of the terms used. The council had collapsed on seeing him hit her for no reason. They are in lots of pain now. I go over to Janice and give her the healing mix I know is for her emotions. In minutes she is better.

Janice says, "When Martha got here, she was covered in bruises and cuts. Also, she had a twisted ankle and a broken rib. That was just the recent injuries. She mentioned that she had many broken bones in the past five years, so I gave her the mix to realign all bones and heal them. Such a mix is felt by the one who made it. I felt every bone in my body except my skull burn as she cried. We are sure the male who hurt her did not risk his attempted murder becoming known. Every injury she suffered was passed off as her being clumsy. She walks to gracefully to be clumsy. Those who knew the truth did what they could to protect lives. Those who did not know better were fooled into thinking Martha was clumsy. No one saw her when she needed the most help."

Warrior says, "If I ever come across that male, I am punishing him for attacking and insulting my princess!"

I say, "I am not even willing to stop you or your clan for what he did to Martha. I do not know if others suffered from him or not. Keep him away from the female mers. My people will not be in danger if I can prevent it. Please excuse me everyone, I have had a long week and my body needs rest."

Everyone nods. I walk out. Martha follows me. I ask, "Want something?"

Martha replies, "I do not know mer ways. I do not know anyone there except you, your parents and Janice. I know you and Janice much more then I know your parents, plus they are the rulers. I am sure they are busy enough. I need to learn. Janice refuses to teach me as I chose warrior. I do not ever want to go through what he did to me again. Help me learn mer ways please."

I say, "Tomorrow Martha. I will take you to warrior training tomorrow. I will introduce you to some of the mers as well. See you in the morning."

With that I enter the royal only hallway. It leads to my parents' room and my room. I go directly to my room. It is nine before I wake up. I usually wake up at five. I am still tired, yet I promised Martha to help her get to the warrior training area and to introduce her to some mers. The area is bright enough at nine so it will be open soon.

I go get Martha and lead her there. Once there I introduce her to other mers. As everyone knows her name now, it is just telling her their names. The instructor says, "Ah, yes. The older child decided to learn to fight. Clan leader says that you needed to know it long ago, yet no one cared enough to help you. Well we care. I warn you though, warrior training is intense, and you will hurt. Has Healer Janice released you from her care? We cannot start your training unless she has."

CHAPTER SEVENTEEN

Warrior Clan Has Pain

Martha says, "I do not know. I want to learn. I do not want to suffer again."

One of the noble warriors, swims off a bit and returns with some bright coral. All of us unmarried mer females except Martha look at it. He is unmarried. It is high interest he declares with grabbing the coral. We wonder who he is interested in. He swims over to Martha and me. Then he says, "Got you some coral Martha. My name is Chris."

Martha says, "Um, hi."

She faces me asking, "What is coral for?"

I say, "You are not ready for it. Mers have a few uses for coral. It makes good food, good medicine, sharp weapons, and as he did an offering of interest. You are not ready for it."

Martha faces Chris then says, "I am sorry. I just got out of a bad situation. I am not ready for anything. Maybe later. Much later."

Some female mers giggle. Martha asks, "What are they laughing about?"

I say, "Some part of you is interested in him, otherwise you would have outright rejected him."

Martha says, "I find him handsome. It is just..."

As she thinks of her recent pass, I feel immense pain coming off her. I grab her and swim up fast. Then I say, "Look Martha. That was you. They feel the pain you went through from your emotions on thinking of it. Until you learn to control the output, you should not think of your past. We stay here until they are better. Healers, the warriors need your help, now. The whole clan is hurting. A brief glimpse of the pain Martha went through."

Soon all healers arrive. They divide into teams of two and help the warriors recover. Chris is last as he is in the most pain. Janice goes over to him asking, "What is wrong brother?"

Chris is in a ball shaking. I say, "Besides me, he was the closest to her. I know what she experienced to have such pain. He does not. At least I do not think he does. He tried to give her coral."

Janice laughs, "Brother, you are crushing on her?"

Chris whimpers, "Mind your own business."

Warrior clan leader says, "Martha, we cannot teach you warrior skills until you can control your emotional output. If we did the whole nation could end up hurting as we did. Go to school as a young mer. That is what you should focus on right now."

Martha looks at Chris saying, "I am sorry."

I move us down. We are now feet from him. I move off. Martha says, "I am sorry. My past hurts. It was physical pain mostly when it occurred. Now it is nearly all emotional. I cannot talk about it yet. I did not know others could feel it when I think of what happened. I am scared of it happening again. I"

Martha drops into silence. Janice hugs her saying, "Back to my office you go. You are not ready to interact with others yet. We have got to get your emotions under control first."

They swim off as Janice's intended and another male healer help Chris. Janice's intended says, "Chris, I do not know what Martha experienced. Janice says that it is awful. Such pain none of us know. Just the brief time she was not held by Janice or Princess, I felt pain, fear, loneliness, and a brief glimmer of desire. That hit when she looked at you. Then Janice grabbed her and there was nothing. She at least has some interest in you."

Chris relaxes. Knowing that everyone was fine now, or soon would be, I swim off. As I swim, I contact my parents letting them know what had occurred and that I was going exploring. As soon as they replied I was allowed to, I shot out of the boundaries and to the surface. I explore more detailed observance of the river path that Martha had shown me. I end at the doctor's home.

CHAPTER EIGHTEEN

Hurting a Jerk... Again

G etting there I knock. It takes her a few minutes to answer. Madeline does not see me as I had hid hearing other voices inside. As she is about to turn around, I call out, Madeline, please come talk with me."

Someone inside asks, "Who is it Madeline?"

Madeline replies, "A friend of mine. I will be back shortly."

She closes the door and walks toward where I had called out from. I lead her a bit away then say, "Martha is almost recovered from her injuries. Just waiting on her rib to finish healing. That and the emotional trauma she went through. She is allowed to stay in my home city as long as she wants. Since it is somewhere that he will never find her, I am sure it will be a while. I let you know as you are the closest friend she ever had. At least in many years. I would have come in except I heard voices I do not know and from Martha's sharing her experiences I am nervous around strangers. Well they might be wondering where you are. I should get going."

Madeline says, "It is actually the royal family and their guards checking on why I have not healed or even attempted to heal the male that abused Martha. He had a visitor two days after you left. The visitor apparently told the king I refused to help him."

I ask, "Are you afraid?"

Madeline says, "It could cost me my job. That would take away my ability to help others. I have no choice; I help him, or many suffer."

I say, "No. You help him, you become just as suppressed as many are. I will help you instead."

With that I toss a cloak over me and go back to her place. Madeline enters before I do saying, "Sorry Sire. Madam Queen. I needed to meet my friend. This is her."

I snap, "No information on me. I do not share or allow others to share about me. My only concern here is Martha. I will not let one who abused another off easy. Martha lives in my home city now. He can suffer as much as he put her through. Also, the warriors of that city, have issues with how he treats others and have already threatened to hurt him if they ever see him. They do not forget their promises. He is in for years of pain."

The king asks, "You have proof of what you charge him with?"

I say, "Madeline refuses to care for him because she spent years caring for Martha from wounds, he inflicted on her."

The male that hurt Martha says, "Liar!"

I flick my wrist saying, "Flea."

He runs at me on his improperly healed ankle with a knife in his hand. Instant warrior training kicks in. I swing my foot out smacking into his ribs. We hear them cracking. I say, "Care for a round four fool? I have no issues with giving out pain to defend myself or others. By the way, I have bad medicines on me. Good medicines heal. Bad medicines make a person extremely sick. I as all doctors where I call home carry both. I know which ones to use and how much to give so you live, but that is not mercy. Try getting near me again and I will make you wish you had never crossed my path. I do not think you will get that chance because you just attacked me in front of your king."

The king says, "I am enjoying the show at this point. You leveled heavy charges and he proved you were right by his actions, yet even my guards cannot react as fast as you do."

I laugh, "Warrior elite training I was required to take. My home city has a good defense team. I never understood why I needed the training until I came across him hitting a female, my friend Martha. Now anytime I see him I am seconds away from dealing out pain. Pardon me got to go."

Then I walk out. In moments, my long stride has me out of their sight. I have the long stride as it makes me faster at swimming as they do, and I had to learn to swim as they did before I could walk among them undetected as someone different then they are. I go back to the river and submerge my face, letting my gills take in the water I need. Meme tells me to be more careful. To carry the water, I need in containers and drink it the way they do. I understand. So, I drop into the deep river and quickly swim back to the ocean. Then I find containers of decent size to carry water in. Meme gathers some containers for me as well.

CHAPTER NINETEEN

Group Rotations

A ll told, I have twenty containers all between three and five inches wide, six to nine inches diameter and with straps to carry over my shoulders. My time is almost up today so I go put them in my thinking space and go home. There I meet alone with Martha, telling her that I had met with Madeline and her former king. The one who hurt her was found guilty. She asks what sentence he was given. I do not know but he currently has a few more broken ribs thanks to trying to attack me. We laugh.

At that moment Janice comes back in saying, "Princess you know it is past visiting hours now and Martha needs rest to recover from the broken bone. It is almost healed though. I am not sure how long it will take for the trauma to subside for her to live happily again. Her trauma level is far beyond anything I have encountered before."

Martha says, "I am actually a lot better now then even this morning. Ann told me the male that hurt me is finally getting justice served to him from his king. I know everything is going to be fine now. I am finally safe."

Janice says, "That is good. It is time for you to get some sleep though. Ann can come back in the morning if she wants. By the way, council meeting tomorrow Ann. Now that we have had time to process what Martha went through, we have things to discuss."

I say, "Alright."

Saying night to Martha, I go home. My parents enter the royal hallway the same time I do. They tell me about the council meeting tomorrow. I nod. Papa says, "The council wants you to attend."

I say, "I figured they want to know more about Martha."

Mom says, "Well, her accidently causing the whole warrior clan pain at once was enough to get them to wonder if her being here is the best thing for everyone."

I sigh, "It is mom. She just needs a bit of time to process everything."

Mom says, "I know. She went through too much for anyone to handle and yet she is somehow still alive. She still has the ability to love. We just have to convince the council of that."

The next day, I visit Martha early. Janice comes in while we visit. She asks, "How are you today Martha?"

Martha replies, "Calm and ready to move forward with my life. What can you tell me about your brother? He seemed interested in me and I think dates would help me adjust to people, especially males again. That one male put me through so much I do not know how to trust yet. I understand most people are not that way, yet the fear of coming across that again is there."

Janice asks, "What is a date?"

I say, "The surface side people are not once only coupled. She thinks in those terms still. What Martha is wondering is if a small group gathering of friends could help her. You know Chris brought her coral."

Janice says, "Which is why she should not ask about him spending time with her. He waits for her acceptance or rejection. I cannot encourage her to spend time with him if she is not committed to a future with him. I will not hurt my brother so."

I say, "I understand Janice. The thing Martha needs the most right now is small group gatherings. Remind your brother that she is just a child still, not even clan trained yet. Perhaps in a couple months she can start clan training. In the meantime, her healing will stall if she does not get to see not all males are that way. Not just their interactions with lots of people, but in smaller settings. Martha, me, a couple married people, a couple of single males. We keep with mer laws. I think rotating between the single males will help Martha relax. Chris will come up. I suggest second or third round, so she has time to process if she cares to know him better for another group gathering with him in it, or not. Also, second or third will not get his hopes up to high if she is not ready."

Janice says, "Fourth or fifth. More groups before will tell him she is not all that into him yet."

Martha says, "I only know his name, looks, and that he is your brother. I am not into anyone currently. I was just asking to get to know others and relax."

I say, "We will put him in the fifth group then. In each group you tell me the thoughts of both singles once they leave us. From that I will decide if they advance to do another group meeting or not. Get some rest Martha, we have a meeting to attend to then will be back later."

Martha sighs. Janice and I go to the council meeting. Warrior brings up the pain Martha had accidently caused his whole clan. Janice says, "She has improved much since then. In only a day her pain dropped radically, and just this morning she asked to do the group rotations. Martha is adjusting. I think Ann telling her that the male who had tormented her was found guilty of his actions speed up her recovery. She is moving forward instead of seeming trapped as she was this time yesterday."

Dad says, "You did not go back there did you Ann?"

I say, "What need would I have of that? We have exceptionally good eyesight, and I am friends with Wela Water. She sometimes tells me things I would not hear otherwise."

Saying that makes them assume I was below the ocean and lower than outsider sight lines. I see no reason to make them worry about me. After all the king of that nation said his elite could not move as fast as I could so I am in little danger there. They do not need the stress. They take it the way I expected. Warrior asks, "Did she really ask for the group rotations?"

Janice says, "In terms she is used to."

Soon after the meeting on if Martha was allowed to stay a mer and live with us ends. They agree she can as she is making progress. I go visit Martha for another hour before going exploring the dry world for four hours. Martha's knowledge on the language was immensely helpful to me. After that I sit in my room and decide who to put into each of the group rotations. All healers are left off as Martha declared desire for warrior training.

The next morning, I go exploring early, realize most outfits further inland are not how I am dressed so I go back to my thinking place and make an outfit similar to the ones I saw females ware there. I finish that as my time this morning ends. I go home and have lunch with my parents before stating, "I am helping Martha in the group rotations. I will be just an observer. It might give me an idea of my own interests in the meantime. Right now, Martha is my priority. After the two hours with her, if it lasts that long, I am going exploring again."

Done letting them know my plans, I go get Martha and then we find a married couple. I say, "Martha has asked for my help in the group rotations. We need a married couple there as law states so. Not as if anyone would try going against law with me in the mix. Still if I do not hold to law, they have right to relax also."

The woman says, "Princess is wise. Yes, we will help you learn what you want."

I say, "I might, however this is Martha's group rotations. She asked. I wait. Exploring is more important to me at this time. Only Martha needs to adjust to mer life, and I can help her do so because I know terms she uses while most do not."

We go get the two males I decided on and find a park table to sit at. The couple sit on one end of the table. Martha sits between the woman and me on one side. The males on the other side. The other end of the table is left open. I explain that Martha wanted to get to know others and their names were drawn first. They introduce themselves to her. The two hours pass decently. Martha says, she cares for the male closest to the married one more then the other. I cross the other one off the list I wrote. Then I go exploring.

Three days later is her next group rotation. Same sort of event. Then another one the same three days after that. The fourth rotation is also the same. The fifth one she looks at Chris a lot. Though Martha asks both questions, it is clear to me that she cares for Chris more. I tap her foot to get her attention and she does not even seem to notice me. After my third try I glance to the married couple and have the woman have her husband ask Chris to walk off with him for a few minutes. I needed to know Martha's reaction. She agrees. Minutes later the man and Chris leave the table. Martha sighs as soon as they are past what she expects they will hear.

Then Martha looks at the other male, a cousin to Chris saying, "I am sorry. I have been rude to you. I do not even remember your name. It seems as if I have wasted your time."

Martha looks to where Chris had followed the man away and sighs. I say, "This rotation is officially over. Leave."

The other single male leaves. I cross his name off. I ask, "Martha were you even interested in getting to know Mike?"

Martha says, "Slightly. I mean I tried, I just…I do not know why but I could not help looking at Chris. His looks appeal to me. Is it normal to feel as if I could do anything?"

I say, "You have been through more then anyone here even wants to imagine. I am sure you could handle a lot. Come on time to get you home. The couple can make sure Chris gets home."

Martha says, "Oh. I was wanting to say goodnight."

I ask, "Are you done with the rotations completely yet?"

Martha replies, "No."

I say, "Not allowed. You cannot tell him goodnight without a full group unless you chose him. I cannot be part of that as he has already declared interest in you in front of me. Only a member of the royal family or the guardians could marry a couple here. I am not allowed to marry you as I have done so much for you already. My being there as you told him goodnight would put me in the wrong. It is best if you just tell the groups goodnight. At least until you decide. How is warrior training coming?"

Martha asks, "Did they make it this hard for you?"

I say, "No. I had it worse as I am a royal and expected to protect the nation. Your training they do not expect to get pass commoner levels. It would shock them for you to advance into noble status."

Martha says, "It would shock me as well. I do not seem to be able to pass even the first course. My muscles are sore every day. This is my new home nation and I intend to fight to keep as many safe as I can, but I got to get stronger to do so."

I ask, "Do commoners even appeal to you at all?"

Martha replies, "I do not know what appeals to me. I know any of the physical traits that surface male had no longer appeal to me. Blond hair as the other single male had. It is not his fault his hair is the same color as the one who hurt me. Still it caused me to have flashbacks when I looked at him, so I focused away from him to make it through."

I say, "I ended it before the two hours as you did not notice me trying to get your attention."

Martha says, "I noticed. I was sure you were trying to tell me not to be rude, I just could not look at him long without having flashbacks. I do not think it would be fair to any of them for me to be trapped in painful memories."

I say, "So all blonds out. See you for your next group rotation."

She goes inside the house made for her. I notice it is still mostly bare. I go home. In my room, I cross off all blonds from the list. It takes an eight of the singles off the list. I crunch the list down. Then I get some sleep. My days are exploring the dry world, small bits at a time, processing the information, getting help from Martha on understanding what I came across and helping her adjust to mer ways, and doing her group rotations.

A few rotations later, Martha removes all black eyed mers from her rotations. Then the next one she has me remove all with curly hair. I condense the list each time. In the times I go exploring I move up the riverbanks, moving inland a bit to avoid houses until I had a chance to observe those who live there. Still as I know the river is a quick way home, and an easy rehydration source I keep the river in my sight.

Three months later, Martha has taken all but three off of her rotation list. Warrior Chris is one of the three. This is her last or almost last rotation before she becomes mated to one of them or remains single for years. Thirty years before she could try again. She has gotten to level three warrior training.

Today is her group rotation. There are the three single males, one married couple, me, Martha and another female friend of hers. Martha sits in the middle. I am on the end. Her other friend is next to the married woman. Chris is center of the male line, a red head on his left by the married male and a brown-haired male on his other side. Chris has black hair. After an hour Martha asks, "What comes after the group rotations?"

Her friend states, "The couple, you and whoever you want talk alone with a royal."

I say, "Not me. This is the last time I join you Martha. Even if you only take one off your rotation list, this is the last time I join you. If you take two off your list, then you can expect to be planning your wedding."

Martha says, "No. I am not ready for that. It is not them. They are nice. It is me. It is what he put me through. Sorry."

CHAPTER TWENTY

Memories and Feelings Not Mine

She runs off. Soon I feel mers in pain. I force a national emotional and knowledge block. Annoyingly, that focuses all emotions and knowledge below my level to me. Martha's extreme pain tops the ranking. Everything else is small. The few she encountered in the minute after she left us are only a slight bit bigger than the rest. They know they had pain but do not realize the reason. They know it is not their own pain but cannot say whose pain they felt. Martha's pain is quickly getting to much for me. I can not let the mers feel it. I cannot let the wateries feel it. Meme! What do I do?

Guardian Meme comes over and wraps me in a hug dragging my now limp body away from the group. I feel so much pain, my body refuses to function. I want the pain flow to stop but I cannot even let go. It feels as if I am being punched, kicked, stabbed and tossed against different things many times. My bones feel as if they are breaking. What is going on? What is happening to me? Why am I here? What did I do to deserve this? Why do my parents not love me? At that I hear guardian say, "Ann, you are experiencing Martha's memories, not your own. Come back to your people. Give her the strength to come back to us as well. Ann! Focus!"

Someone's else has these memories? They are not mine? They did not happen to me. I know who. A friend. Martha. I focus hard on the images of my getting her away from there, her joining the mers, her making friends here, the healing she went through, and the fact that the male who had hurt her is no longer able to as he attacked me in front of his king. In moments, I feel Martha crying. Yet it no longer hurts the way it did mere minutes ago. It is relief now. Everyone else's emotions gradually become about equal to Martha's. At that point I release the knowledge flow. I am drained and tired, yet I need to check on Martha. Guardian says, "Stay still for a few minutes Ann. Let the people recover."

I ask, "Recover?"

Meme replies, "You took from all their energy to keep the knowledge and emotion flow locked so they did not get hurt."

A few minutes later I go find Martha. She is at the edge of the city. She has no idea about the creepy fish that guard our border. I know she is not ready to consider marriage as that is what triggered her memories and caused her to run. Meme and I lift her up and take her to her home. There is a small sofa, a tiny coffee table, a couple chairs and a rug in the living area. The dining area has four chairs around a small table. The kitchen is as basic as when it was made. The bedroom is as well.

Most of her place is the basic way it was built for her. It saddens me as she has nothing personal to add to any area. After we set her on her bed I glance in her closet. I had to know if she got anything. There is only the outfits mom had bought for her. Mom and I had picked them out together. Something she might be used to. It means she is not wanting to stay here, is not adjusting how well I thought she was, is planning on running, or just unsure of our currency. I hope it is the currency issue. She is the first mortal friend I have. In fact, right now she is the only mortal friend I have.

I have to make myself a health realignment that evening. I sleep late the next day because of it. I missed school time. Us older mers only have class once every three months. Everyone understands if I miss class I am in royal duties, but I think it is wrong to schedule anything in a time you know you are to be somewhere else. Oversleeping from an extreme overload of emotions is not over scheduling though. I go explain to my parents what had occurred incase my teachers stopped by then go to Martha's home.

After I knock, Martha takes a few minutes to answer. She sighs, "Come in Ann. I am just about to have tea. Care to join me?"

I go in asking, "Tea?"

Martha says, "On land it was made with a plant leaves and boiled water poured over it. Basically, a flavored water. My tea is the one thing he never took away from me. He could not as I grew the plants in our enclosed yard. It kept the animals from eating them as easily. He could not keep me from being clean, so I had water. I guess I had tea to help me stay hidden. I could at least tend to my plants while I recovered. That medicine I was given when I came here, I think of as an unexperienced tea maker's attempt to make me feel comfortable. I just cannot seem to give up tea. Here I am trying to see what will make a flavoring I am used to."

I say, "I doubt any could as we cannot boil water. How are you doing?"

CHAPTER TWENTY-ONE

Removal of a Forced Document

Martha says, "You mean after yesterday? I am fine. I had not realized that I was so close to marrying. I mean I used to dream about falling in love and getting married. After being forced to marry him even though the mers do not consider it valid, it is still a valid document there, and I have been left scared of the pain repeating. I can not marry until the king of the land folk demolishes that document. It has to be voided before I can even consider marrying. The three mers we were with are nice. Those three, the married couple, you and Fina helped me know I can have a normal life again. I can feel something besides pain again. I want to move on. However, I need that marriage document ended. There are three ways for it to be over. One my death recorded there. Two a divorce. Three the document nulled."

I ask, "Nulled?"

Martha replies, "Found to be untruthful in the statements on it. I was fifteen. So, my parents had to sign that they had no issues with him becoming my husband. I wish they had loved me the way the mers love their families and each other. Maybe I would not have suffered then. I see the mers care about each other. They genuinely care. Even if they cannot stand each other they care enough to help each other. It is something I have no idea how to process. I am glad to be here."

I question, "Why is your home so basic?"

Martha says, "Saving for something. Also, I still am learning your currency."

I say, "We will help you learn. Anything you need?"

Martha states, "The voiding of the marriage document. I want… I want a date."

I laugh. Soon after I leave. I go let my parents know I am exploring then go do so. I go directly to Madeline's place and knock. When she answers I say, "Martha is doing well."

Madeline says, "That is good. What is on your mind?"

I say, "You have met her parents?"

Madeline says, "I take it you want to meet them?"

I say, "I think I need to understand why they forced her to marry her attacker."

Madeline says, "No answer could be reason enough to hurt your child."

I say, "I know. Lead way."

Madeline walks into the forest some. I follow her marking the trees with fish bones as I go. Ten minutes later we come to a small clearing. A house is in the center of the clearing. Madeline knocks. An older woman answers then confused asks, "Why are you here doc?"

Madeline says, "Martha is gone."

The woman gasps, "No! He will kill her. Then he will kill us. We must find her."

I say, "Good luck with that. Martha is completely safe. Did you realize he raped her before their marriage? Did you know he beat her until she barely lived many times? Did you know that she wonders why you do not love her?"

At that the woman cries, "We do love our girl. It hurt to hear her say she had been hurt. We confronted him. He told us that we either forced her to marry him or he would kill her in front of us before killing us. Though the king would throw him into the dungeons for years, he would be alive, and we would not be. He has connections to insure anyone who knew otherwise would not say any different then what he did, so he would act as if he just came upon our dead family. No one would be punished. The only thing we could do is sign her wedding document."

I ask, "What happens to that document if his threat against your lives became known?"

She replies, "It is void. We cannot void it as long as Martha is with him. She is not safe there. I know she is not. We did what we could to save her life. I do not even know who you are or how you know Martha, let alone why I share with you."

I say, "Martha left him. She ran with my help. He cannot keep up with me even when I was carrying Martha. I broke one of his ankles, one of his wrists and many ribs. Madeline does not help him recover."

Madeline says, "After you left last time the king had him arrested and thrown into the dungeons for twenty years. It was far to satisfying to hear him scream when your foot connected to his ribs. Extremely satisfying to hear him protest that you were lying as the king ignored him and took him away under heavy guard detail. I laughed for hours. Martha deserves better than that. She is such a sweet lass."

I say, "That means there is a good chance of the king you serve believing you when you tell him your story. Martha wants dates but she will not move forward until she knows she is not held in that document anymore. Your task is now to get that document voided. You can bring me the proof in Madeline's home."

The woman says, "We would really love to see our daughter again."

I say, "If she wants to see you, I will see if that could be arranged. I do not know if she will though, you did after all force her to marry someone who had hurt her. I do not see why you didn't just grab essentials and run."

The woman says, "We believed he would find us before we could ever get out of the nation. Then we would die."

I ask, "Ever consider asking the sea for help? No, you would not. Three days of Martha asking, and the sea got to wondering why she wanted help. At that time, I was just exploring the coastline. Martha called out to the sea. My ally and I heard her. We saw him hit her. Martha now lives in a sea town."

The woman says, "You talk strange. It will take me a bit to get to the castle, convince the king to meet with me and get back. What is your name? How will I let you know if I get the document voided or not?"

I say, "I do not care how long it takes you. My name is unimportant to you. I check with Madeline occasionally so I will get the message if you tell her. Until that document is voided, I will not even ask Martha if she wants to see you."

Then I walk back to the path where we had come from and remove the fish bone markers. My time is to close to being done to explore further, so as Madeline catches up, I ask her to get everyone that she could to testify against that document, or that male's attitude. After she agrees I go home.

Nearly no one sees me in this dry world because I move so quietly, and sneak pass the houses. It is as if they do not realize anyone spies on them. Guardians have reminded me that magic picks up on things nonmagics have no way of knowing. Quiet bliss causes them to be deceived easier than the noisy thoughts I have always flowing to me. My people's concerns and happiness. It all comes all the time. I can lower the volume but not completely get rid of it. That will only happen when I pass rule to someone else. Anything I have learned and experienced will at that time be copied into the royal archives for the future generations to know. Once read, it will be remembered.

At the yearly national dinner that night my parents ask, "What did you learn from the sea today Ann?"

Knowing that none of them knew I was above the ocean or even near the surface and it would scare them to learn it, besides the guardians have final say and granted me permission, so I just reply, "That our sea is good to us. It provides us with all we need. That is why we care for it."

I do obey my parents and if their council is united in the decision, I would obey them also. However, I will not give up something the guardians said I could have or do. Therefore, only stating I am learning our sea is good to us is all I need to do. I do not need to stress them about how far I go to learn such. I really do not need to stress my people. They truly do not know just how good the sea is to us.

The sea does not just give up its secrets to the dry world people. Perhaps they do not understand it. It does not really matter. The sea is good to the mers and the wateries. We do not waste what it gives us. Even the coral Warrior Chris took from the sea was used. He made a few weapons from it. I have never made weapons from anything, as I do not understand the need we have here so far from everything for a warrior clan. Instead I trained my body to be my greatest asset. Toned to the core. Pure muscle and bone. Yet I have heard some single males call me beautiful. They do not say it to my face or anywhere they think I am near, but I have snuck up on some that had said, "Princess is so beautiful."

I punished them for gossiping about me. Had they the courage to actually tell me they would not have been punished. I do not know if they were trying to get me to personally notice them or not. I do not care. If you want to talk about someone, make sure they will hear it. That is my expectations.

Just then Wela comes in. My father asks, "Why are you here young Water?"

Wela replies, "Mer king, I wanted to visit my friend Ann."

My father nods slightly giving the permission for her to come to me. Wela stands beside me then says, "Ann asked for information from a couple. They got it. Something mentioned about Madeline."

I say, "Thank you. I think my parents would enjoy your leaving our yearly gathering."

Wela nods and leaves. Mom asks, "Who is Madeline?"

I reply, "An acquaintance."

Martha asks, "Is it the doc?"

I reply, "Just some low skilled healer."

Martha asks, "What did she want?"

I say, "It is not what she wanted but what you asked for, concerning a certain false document. It was voided. I am going to meet Wela tomorrow for the proof."

Martha shrieks, "I love you!"

I laugh, "Of course you do. You are a mer."

Everyone laughs. Chris wonders, "What document, if I might ask?"

Martha drops her head. I say, "It does not matter. How is your warrior training coming Martha?"

At that she looks up again smiling. Martha replies, "If I were strong enough to get surface side, I would give someone as many broken bones as I suffered. I would do it all at once then laugh in his face. Then I would walk away letting him suffer for as long as he could. As it is, I hope he suffers many years. Just as he put me through many years in suffering."

I say, "Let me see your strength then."

CHAPTER TWENTY-TWO

Forgiveness

Martha says, "Princess I am not going to fight you."
I say, "Not even if I entertain thoughts of bringing you to talk to your parents?"

Since I was feet from her as I said that she swings at me. My parents did not hear what I said. I say, "I take it you hate them."

Martha swinging at me again says, "Naturally! They do not love me. Why should I care to see them? You know it!"

I am dodging her punches easily. I decide to irritate her, so I say, "I invited them for a visit."

Bam! I land on my rear. Warrior clan leader stands. I say, "Be calm. My joke was poorly taken. I wanted to see if she actually could defend herself now. I could not see her helpless again. It hurt too much to see it once. I asked for the fight remember. I knew that would provoke her. It did not hurt as much as some people have done when they were too filled with anger to see who they were against anymore. Still far better then when she joined us. What rank did she reach?"

Clan leader sits muttering, "Low noble. I still intend to punish her for attacking you."

I say, "No. I already decided on a punishment. You know it would be far worse than anything you could deal out."

He laughs. I face my parents asking, "Might I have Wela bring a couple here? I think it would be the final thing for Martha to release the pain she has went through. I take full responsibility."

Meme shows up and places her hand on my shoulder. Not even Papa would argue with her agreement with me. Papa asks, "What couple?"

I say, "Might I go exploring Meme?"

Everyone gasps as none of them have that name, so they know I addressed a guardian by name. Meme says, "Keep your time frames. They are not to come here. We will meet them in a neutral area you can show them to in a week or two. Not sure exactly when. Still talking with the others."

I nod. Then I leave the mer nation and go surface side. I go immediately to Madeline's home. Martha's parents are there waiting. They give me the document with voided stamped clearly across it, signed and sealed by their king. They ask again to see their daughter. I reply, "In a week or two. Do not ask for a specific date. I am still talking it over with superiors. I will come get you when it is time."

The woman says, "Thank you."

Martha's father says, "It means a lot to us."

I say, "I do not care how much it means to you nor for your thanks. I do so as you have gotten Martha freed from a marriage, she should have never been in to begin with. Do not expect her to take kindly to either of you. She suffered for years from your actions and lack of courage."

Then I go home. It is dinnertime now. I walk right over to Martha and drop the document in front of her. Then I go hug my mom telling her how much I love her and papa always showing me how much they care about me. Mom hugs me tightly. I smile although I feel embarrassed, at least I never doubt their love. When mom releases me, I sit down in my seat beside her. I glance over all my people then see Martha staring at the document she has opened. I feel her shock and delight. Suddenly she jumps up, runs to me without permission and hugs me.

A mummer goes around questioning her actions and if she will be punished. I say, "I guess that is you forgive me for inviting your parents to meet with you, more as promising them they would get to."

Martha says, "I guess. I mean I am free! I can... well a date would be wow."

I laugh. Janice asks, "You want to resume the group rotations? Were you not down to three?"

Martha replies, "I was down to three. I do want to continue the group rotations."

The red-haired male asks, "You going to run out on us again?"

Martha says, "I was dealing with my outsider past. I might have issues from it for a while. Do you think I would be worth trying even if I were to run often?"

He replies, "Not to me you are not."

The brown-haired male says, "Not that into you."

Chris stands up and walks over to her. He holds out two small weapons saying, "I made these from the coral I offered to you. I find that even though I only offered as your physical appeal to me then, I still want to offer them to you. Would you pledge yourself to me?"

Martha asks, "Ann, what do I do?"

I reply, "That is your choice. You can accept the weapons and become engaged to him. Or you can reject the weapons and as everyone else was removed from the list you would have to wait thirty years to try the group rotations again. By then you would be healed from your hard past I am sure. The choice is entirely yours. What do you want?"

There is stillness for a moment before Martha touches his hands and places them near his heart. Then she tosses her arms around his neck. If his hands were not crossed over his heart and squished between them, I am sure he would hug her back. Papa congratulates them on their engagement. That is followed by mom and me then everyone else. I say, "I am sure your parents would want to meet your betrothed."

Martha says, "It would actually help me deal with meeting them."

Since it is late, dinner ends shortly after that. The next day, I spend time in my thinking place. Meme shows me where to take Martha's parents to so to meet with her, me, my parents, Chris and his parents. I nod and ask about when I should show them there. Meme says, "In two days. Tomorrow tell them to plan for a week away. The day after that show them there. I will get the mers to meet them on that small island."

The next day, I tell Martha's parents that I would show them to where they would get to see their daughter tomorrow and that they might be gone a week. They rush home to pack for a week away. I go exploring for a bit. The trees are getting closer together. The river is curving. I am out of time.

After lunch, I go get Martha's parents and we row to the island Meme had shown me. Docking on the island, I say, "Martha, my parents, a friend of hers and that friend's parents will be joining us sometime soon."

Martha's mother asks, "How soon?"

I say, "Relax. They will arrive when they arrive."

Two days later, Meme leads Martha and the others over. Meme leaves. Papa says, "Ann, introduce the couple."

I say, "Pa, this is Martha's parents, Madam Niccole, and Sir Nick."

Martha says, "Yea, I did not matter to them."

Chris asks, "Please explain."

Martha sighs, "They forced me to marry someone who had hurt me. I was trapped in pain until Ann rescued me."

Niccole says, "After you told us what happened, we confronted him. He threatened to kill you in front of us then kill us before claiming he had come across all three of us and tried to save us. We did not know anyone to help us escape with you or where to go in a hurry, so we had no choice to save your life we had to act as if we agreed to the union. That is the reason the document was able to be voided. I am so sorry I lacked courage to even try running."

Martha states, "I was beaten daily. Many times, I barely lived. I would not let him touch me willingly, so I was beat. Every bone in my body neck down was broken at one point or another. He… often. Tea was the only thing I had left. I grew the plants in his enclosed yard and had the water as he did not want me stinking when he had anyone over. It was very satisfying to hear Ann crack his bones, giving him a small fraction of the pain, he put me through. I am glad not to be anywhere I have to be concerned about him hurting me anymore."

Chris asks, "He what often Martha?"

Martha looks pained. Nick says, "He raped her. We confronted him on his raping our girl and were made to turn her over to him."

Tears flow down Martha's face. Chris hugs her saying, "Oh, my sweety, come on. My sister could help you. Her husband could give me something to help my emotions because I want to find that male and castrate him."

Martha laughs, "That would be something funny to watch. More to do so myself. I only wish we could make him go through it as many times as he hurt me that way."

Chris says, "It still would be mercy. Nice meeting you sir, madam."

They dive into the water together. His parents laugh. His mother asks, "How long do you think it will be before she wants our son's touch Jack?"

Jack replies, "Not long Deann, not long. Given what she went through, I am surprised she even asked to do group rotations."

Niccole asks, "Group rotations?"

I reply, "Dates. Small group dates."

Nick asks, "You mean she is dating that boy?"

I laugh, "No. They are past dating. He proposed to her. She accepted. They will be married whenever they set a day to do so."

Papa says, "Do not stay out to long Ann. Air is drier than our people are used to."

I say, "I know papa. Drier climate. I need to get them home. I will be home soon."

My parents and Chris's parents swim off. Niccole asks, "Why did they swim? Where to?"

I say, "We live in a moist climate. Swimming here feels better. Closer to what we are used to. They will swim back to where the connection home is. Come on, your home awaits."

Niccole says, "You still talk funny. What nation are you from?"

I say, "Does not matter."

Nick says, "We are glad we got to see our daughter. Her being happy is a bonus. We had not been able to see her since we were forced to give her away."

I say, "It is over with now."

CHAPTER TWENTY-THREE

Feeling Alone

Then I ride with them back to their home shore. They head off. I dive when there is no one around. Soon I make it home. My parents are glad I am safe and suggest none of us tell anyone else about the land visit. I nod having no intentions of doing so. Martha, Chris and his parents accept that as a command. Chris has his arm around Martha's waist. She is leaning toward him. Chris says, "Sire, when is the soonest you would allow Martha and I to get married?"

My father replies, "A month so she can have any ceremony she wants."

Martha says, "Sometimes I feel as if I am living two separate lives."

I say, "Because you have. An outsider life and a mer life."

Martha states, "That makes me feel as if I am dreaming all the time. What is real anymore?"

Chris states, "It all is. The bad past led you to us and me. I say, if this is a dream, I do not want to wake up."

Martha says, "I will enjoy this dream as long as it lasts."

Chris states, "I hope you enjoy all three thousand or so years of it."

Martha is stunned. Then she kisses Chris. Papa says, "Fine married.

You can still have an event if you want, but the nation recognizes your union to Chris."

That stuns Martha more. I say, "Martha did not realize marriage law is first kiss between a couple when both freely give it."

Martha says, "No. In that case, I want to do this knowing what it means."

She kisses Chris again. I leave. Alone. I am so alone. I swim to my thinking place. Meme hugs me asking me what is wrong. I say, "Martha got married. While I am happy for her, I am so alone. I know couples share more then even friends do. I have so little friends. My people will always remember I am their princess. Martha was different but now that she is married, I expect she will learn from him how to respond to situations. While I am glad the guardians treat me as a friend and allow me to treat them so, part of me always remembers they are guardians. I am sorry if it upsets them. It is just what I do."

Meme says, "We are not upset. You cannot change how they react to you because of your rank just as you cannot change how you react to us because of our rank. That is why you explore so much. It is why you go to the land so much. Boss has told us you are safe even past our care. We do not know why you are special to boss."

Trembling I ask, "Might I meet?"

CHAPTER TWENTY-FOUR

Guardian Without Gender

Meme says, "Zeffron, the youth Merth Ann asks to meet you."

Soon a female with, long wavy brown hair, green eyes and light skin shows up. Meme faces her saying, "Boss."

I drop my eyes in recognition of the authority this stranger has over me. I say, "Guardian, why am I special to you?"

Zeffron replies, "I am genderless Ann. You can use my name. I suggest you keep such to a minimum though. I would also allow your descendants to call me by name. You are in the royal bloodlines of the magic nations. That is reason enough to make sure you are safe. My ability to keep you safe exceeds Meme's and her equals. You will not hear from or see me often, but I will help you if you call out to me. Well, I must go. I have things to do."

Just that fast Zeffron is gone. Meme says, "Hurry home Ann, your time is almost up. Boss can move through time."

Tired anyways without being sure why I am tired I obey. I sleep all the next day. The day after that, I go exploring again. I think my parents have accepted that I know the risks of exploring, understand those risks, and would be safe. I do not ask and do not volunteer information to them. I know they are concerned about me all the time. Especially after what Martha experienced that I shared with them.

I know I get further from home every time I explore. I just simply have a need to learn. Maybe the lack of friends drives me to learn more. Possible. I still follow the river inland. Every day the trees get closer together. Any time I hear anyone I hide and watch them unwilling to risk talking to them incase they are the way Martha's forced union was.

It has been nearly two years since I first came to the surface and walked the beach. The forest is thick here. I can barely see a few dozen feet in front of me, even with my great eyesight. I could run this distance in two days. I swim upstream until I reach my fish marker from where I left off the last time I explored then head inland on foot. When time nears an end, I place my marker down and swim home. I turn sixteen today and my parents are throwing me a party tonight.

CHAPTER TWENTY-FIVE

Buying a Human Debt

I look up as a bird had made a sound and I did not know what had done so. I do not know the bird and will be sure to ask Martha about it later. As I look back down, I see some peaks over the treetops. A building. Must be a castle, it is more spaced out then the simple buildings I have come across. People… I am not sure about meeting a lot of people, but it would teach me more about their culture. I decide since it is near a lot of people, it is worth the risk. I follow the sight of the peaks into the forest.

When I notice my last water container is low, I place my fish marker down and turn around intending to pick up here tomorrow. I do not see the river. I am lost! I promised to stay safe and I am lost. My parents and people will be so worried. There is nothing I can do except continue on to the castle. Maybe I can get someone to show me back to the river. The other option is just waiting here until I dehydrate, starve or am found. Of those three possibilities, dehydrating seems the most probable. So, I face my fish marker, pick it up and walk in that direction.

An hour passes, I am so thirsty. So, lost. How am I going to get home? Would I get water in time to prevent dehydration? Would I even have any help so far from the water without calling out to big boss? The land slopes slightly up so I know I am on the side of a mountain, a sharp incline in the land. I come to a clearing. I see the city around the castle I have been looking at the peaks of inside some walls in the clearing. The place is massive. How will I find help here?

I look more at the clearing. One tree grows there. It has something growing on it. A male is sitting at its base eating one of the things that grow from the tree with one hand and drawing with his other hand. I wonder what he draws. I do not dare get close enough to find out without knowing how he treats others. My body again complains of a need for water.

To scared to just approach a lone stranger, I stand there observing him. He seems about my age. Some other male comes over to the one sitting below the tree from the city. They talk to each other, but I am to far to hear the conversation. I do see the pleasant interaction between them. It is enough with my extreme thirst and being lost to make up my mind to take a chance for the help I need. Once the other person leaves, I wait three minutes then go over to the male sitting down. I say, "Pardon me, could I get a drink and directions to the river?"

He replies, "Sure. First let me lead you into the town around the castle here. There is a water fountain so you can fill your canteens and I will get you lunch. I imagine you are hungry."

I nod. We go into the city. I am extremely nervous. He shows me to the fountain. I sit on its edge. He walks off while I fill my water containers. I guess these are what he calls canteens. I drink one slowly to fool the people here. They are part of this dry world after all. Then I refill it. I strap it to the rest as he walks back. I am just biding time to get away, so I do not cause unneeded questions. I would not know how to answer them safely. He hands me a plate of I do not know what. I assume it is the dry people's food. I see fish. That I at least recognize. At least the shape is fish. I smell it. Different then I am used to, but it smells as cod. I eat that first. Strange yet I do not mind it prepared this way. I pass the plate back saying, "I am not sure if I can handle foods here. Trying one thing at a time is best. That cod was good."

He asks, "So you enjoy fish?"

I reply, "On occasion. Please I am lost and want to get home."

He says, "This way to the river then."

Following him I pay close attention to what landmarks he points out. He mentions something about a tiger pack in this forest. I just grunted. I will ask Martha about that. Seeing the river, I slightly relax. I will get home safely. I will be able to keep my promise. He says, "I will walk you home, so you don't get lost again."

Terror swamps me. There is no way I would lead him to my home. I just met him. I do not know him. I am not going to get lost again. How could I explain to him that it was not safe to do so? How could I get away and go home? Oh, please just let me leave alone. I cannot rehydrate if others are near. I feel my body shaking. He says, "It is fine if you don't want me to. Are you sure you will be OK and get home safely?"

I relax. He is truly kind. I say, "I know where I am headed. It will not take me long to get there. Thank you for being so kind and helping me."

Though I see his confusion at my words I head down river. I walk as I do not dare let him follow me into the waterways. I takes small drinks of my water as I walk. I am so glad he withdrew his suggestion of walking me home. I would not be able to fully rehydrate if he stayed close and I was extremely needing to. After I reach the curve in the river, I turn around. I am not followed. Good! I down all my water then I dive, and swim home, dropping off the canteens at my thinking space. After I check in with my parents, I go visit Martha. I ask, "Martha what is a tiger?"

Martha says, "A wild animal. Similar to a cat, except much, much bigger."

I ask, "Cat? Is that similar to catfish?"

Martha says, "Show you images. You would understand better seeing them."

I open the knowledge flow between us. I see the differences she does not know how to tell me. Then I ask about what was on the plate that male handed me. She shows me apples, berries specifically raspberry and bread. She calls it all good. Then mentions she is not sure how a mer would handle any of it. She also shows me other berries, strawberries, blueberries, and blackberries. I show her an image of the tree with things growing on it. I ask about what it is.

Martha tells me the tree is a fruit tree and the things growing on it are pears. She mentions she enjoyed them as a land person. She also mentions there are other fruit trees and shows me images of apple trees, peach trees, orange trees, and grapefruit trees. I ask what bread is. Martha shows me a plant she calls wheat be crushed into something she calls flour, mixed with a whiteish substance called milk from an animal called a cow, a couple eggs from a bird type creature they call a chicken, and something called yeast. Martha cannot explain that one to me. Then that mix is put in a pan and heated for half an hour until it is brownish. Martha assures me it is edible but that seems really weird to me.

The next two weeks I spend in my thinking space going over all the information the kind male had given me even without realizing he did. I think over his kindness, what I had learned from him, the information Martha had given me on top of that and the kind male's appearance. I have one main word to describe him. Yum. He has a tanned complexion, deep red toned eyes and dark hair. Why am I even thinking of him as Yum? He is a dry person after all, and I am and will probably always be a part of the sea. I mean we cannot be much more different. Still, he appeals to me. Why does he appeal to me? It must be his kindness when I needed it. That is, it. I probably would think of anyone as yum in that case. It just happened to be him. Plus having no friends outside of the guardians, it makes since that I would be attracted to a male that treated me as a friend especially when we are strangers. It is not him personally, it is the kindness he showed me.

Even though I know it is his kindness to a stranger that attracts me to him, I cannot avoid thinking about him and his appearance try as I might not to. Every time I think of the things, I learned on that land exploration, I think of the kind male I describe as yum. I guess I should go thank him for helping me find my way, giving me food and water. Yes, that should get him out of my mind. After all it would never work between a sea person and a land person. We are to different. I wonder if he thinks of me. I wonder if he does think of me, why his opinion of me even matters to me? I mean there is nothing, perhaps not even physical attraction between us. What could ever be? Would he accept my magic if he knew? No, he cannot know. I cannot tell him. Guardians warned me against letting the dry people learn of my magic. They fear magics and some of them would kill me for it. I did not choose to be born so. Still I enjoy my life. Much better than the way Martha lived as a dry person.

I keep up my usual out of the mer boundaries every day, so my parents do not question me about things I am not ready to discuss yet. I just go sit in my thinking space. Meme asked me if I had a lot to think over at the beginning of the week. I nodded. The guardians leave me alone unless I ask for them now. I do not ask. I am not ready to tell them what is on my mind, let alone who, especially as I do not know his name even. Sir yum. Great. He is on my mind again. I make sure to keep my time frames, to keep my parents and people from worrying about me.

After the two weeks, I think it is time I go thank him, so I go to the tree I saw him at, pick a pear and sit down trying the fruit. It is strange. I do not think I care for it. I do not know where in the city to find him, I do know he at least visits this tree. I will wait here as long as I can each day to thank him. It is early morning, in fact the sun has only been up for an hour, yet I am here. My parents do not ask anymore how long I will be exploring. They know it is close to four hours.

Minutes after I sit down, the kind male I think of as yum shows up. I smile on seeing him without meaning to. He smiles looking at me. Oh, wow. His smile makes him even more yum. I tell myself off about my obsessive thoughts over him, after all I do not even know his name. He comes over saying, "Hi my name is Matt."

Yum, Matt. Even his name sounds good too me. Fishes Ann! You just met him. Why do you think of him as yum? Crazy fish girl. My thoughts still refuse to go past yum. I just reply, "I am Ann."

Matt says, "You enjoy pears? It is my favorite fruit."

I was going to say that it was nasty, yet at his words I take a big bite just to keep that yum smile on his face. Even his body is yum, toned, strong, and yum. I feel as if my heart has been mildly hit by a stingray. Matt is a danger to my heart anyways. I should thank him and leave. Instead, I say, "I have not had it before. It is different then I am used to. Not sure about it. Anyways, I wanted to thank you again for your help Matt."

His name even rolls easily out of my mouth. I wonder how his tastes. If it tastes as pear then pear could easily make a top food choice. I do not even know how to process what I think of him. Am I just attracted to his kindness and looks? Is it something else, something deeper? How could I know? I cannot ask my parents or their council to many questions without subjecting myself to many questions I do not have answers to myself.

Matt says, "You seemed confused when I said there were tigers in the forest. Why?"

Drat his paying attention. I reply, "Never seen one."

Matt says, "I will introduce you to the pack leader. That way you will be safe coming here. First off, we need meat, raw meat. Lots of it. Come on."

We go into the city and to a shop that sales meat. The smells make me sick. It has fish smells as well. I follow that smell over to many dead fish behind something see through. I place my hand on that. A dry person on the other side says, "No touching the glass miss."

Matt says, "I will by whatever she wants from there."

I look at him. Though I know it might cause questions, I must atone for the lives taken from the sea without the sea's permission. I know there was no permission as they just sit here smelling at different stages of uh. I say, "I do not care for the fish being displayed here. Not this way. I want no fish on display here. Could you get that to happen?"

Matt says, "You ask a lot Ann."

I say, "No fish on display that are just dead. In my culture, if we want to eat fish, we catch only what will be eaten in a few hours. Every other fish is allowed to live. We use whatever we get. There is no waste. The bones are not even wasted. This barters me. So much waste."

Matt says, "Bag up all the fish. I am sure tiger pack will eat it."

The other dry person says, "I do not get how you stay safe while alone in the forest. That tiger pack is dangerous."

He starts bagging up the fish. Matt says, "Why do you think I carry meat out there often? The forest is on three sides of this city and the mountain cliff is on the other, everyone coming here or leaving must go through the forest."

The other male says, "That is why we have so few visitors. I am surprised a path is not cleared through the forest."

Matt says, "Disrupting the tiger hunting grounds. Would you enjoy your home being disrupted as you are suggest doing?"

The other male says, "They are animals! One would think you could tell the difference between people and animals!"

Matt says, "I know the difference. Do you? Even animals have feelings."

Then Matt places his hands on the display cover many times. The shop person says nothing to him about not touching the display. Matt pays for the fish, telling the person to enjoy cleaning the glass, refuses to be charged for the labor it will cost and pulls me out of the store. He has about twenty bags of fish on his arms. People scrunch their noses at the fish smell as we walk past. I say, "Why does he think animals do not care if their homes are destroyed?"

Matt says, "Some people just think that way."

I say, "That is simply wrong. They have families too. People should work with the animals not against them. Everything is easier that way."

Matt says, "Some people do not understand that."

I say, "We do."

We walk into the forest together. Matt calls out, "Tiger, food for your pack."

Suddenly we are surrounded by the animals that Martha showed me are called tigers. One steps toward us. Matt dumps a bag. The tiger moves closer to Matt very slowly. Then it picks up a fish and tosses it to another tiger. This continues until the fish are gone. Matt dumps another bag. The process repeats until all fish in all bags are gone. The tigers ate them all. They do not go to waste. Only the bones are left. The tiger closest to us digs a hole with its foot. The rest pick up the bones and drop them into the hole. Then one buries the bones in the dirt. Matt says, "This is Ann. She is my friend and asked we deliver fish to your pack today."

I ask, "Will it allow me to touch it?"

Matt replies, "I have never tried."

I slowly reach toward the tiger closest to me. It shows me its teeth. I stop. It relaxes. I understand it is scared of me. I just say, "Nice to meet you all."

Matt says, "Getting late. You should get home."

I look at my fish movement timer and realize I have just enough time to get home without stressing anyone. I say, "See you soon Matt."

Then I run toward the river. Once there I make sure I am alone and dive. I reach home as my scheduled time. My breathing is not labored as I asked Wela to help adjust the pressure differences. I got to the higher pressures fast and sunk from the shock. After I rest for an hour, I swim out of the mer boundaries again. Once pass their limits, I say, "Wela. I know I owe you. What do you want?"

Wela shows up minutes later. She says, "Craft me something from one of your scales."

I touch her showing her the image of the fish in the shop asking,

"What do I owe for them? Their lives bought me safety in a land area."

Wela says, "Fish are your father's domain. You would have to ask him."

I say, "Please Wela, take on the debt. Only the guardians and wateries know I go surface side. I do not want my parents to panic. Please Wela, what would I owe you to take on that debt whatever it is?"

Wela says, "Your laws state that a scale could be traded to avoid any punishment. Does it not?"

I say, "It does."

Wela says, "Then I want a full scale as I took punishment from you. That does not mean I want punished either. We will consider it an even trade. You will get your scale back soon."

I hand her the scale thanking her. Then I craft her a case with another. I say, "Case is for your help earlier today."

She nods. We part ways. I go home. An hour later lunch is served. Ten minutes into the meal Wela come in. She says, "King Mer, I purchased a debt. Outsiders had owed it. What is owed?"

My father asks, "What are we talking about?"

Wela tosses the image I had showed her up. Every mer starts talking about the mass loss of our fish. They wonder why she would purchase the debt from the outsiders. Papa says, "Silence! Her reasons matter not. It is done. Our laws state that for every fish wasted a year shall be spent in our cages. I counted two hundred. As the Water people clean the water, we mers need I will discount that by half. One hundred years in our cages. Are you sure you want to purchase the outsider's debt?"

Smiling Wela says, "It is done. The debt is mine. I am also aware that I have this."

Wela holds out my scale saying, "Ann gave it to me after I did a favor for her."

Papa says, "Very well the punishment is Ann's now. Give her back her scale."

As Wela hands me my scale, mom says, "Mers have right to ask for the fish Merco. Ann is one of us."

Papa says, "That is right. Twenty hours in the cages Ann to clear Wela's debt."

I nod, "Yes sire."

CHAPTER TWENTY-SIX

Mer Jail Cells

That is far better than I deserve having originally occurred the debt myself. Papa leads me to the cages below our city. Then to the toughest area where no magic can be used an opens the door to the toughest cell. I walk in. Papa locks the door saying, "See you tomorrow Ann."

There is nothing in this cage. I cannot even use magic. I cannot move into my mer form. There are no windows. No furniture. No light. No sound. No animals. I am completely alone with nothing. So, my thoughts turn to meeting Matt. Handsome Matt. He is so yum. I again wonder how he tastes. I wonder if I could ever bring him to the mer nation. I wonder if he thinks of me. I wonder if he cared for me. I barely know him; I should not be dwelling on him.

My thoughts go round in circles centered on Matt and his appeal to me. I lose tract of time, unable to see my fish tracker. I fall asleep hungry. I wake up hungry. Since I normally wake up at five, I am nearly sure it is five. That means I have five hours left to clear my debt. My thoughts turn into wondering how Matt is doing. How he might touch the woman he is married to or would marry. The thought that he might be married hurts powerfully. I realize I do not know if he is single or taken. I need to know now. After a bit I feel sick. Knowing it is my need to know if Matt is married, I know there is nothing even Janice could do. I need to get to the surface. The sooner the better.

Somehow, I have learned to tell the passage of time even without seeing it. I have one hour left if I am right. However, I am so sick from not knowing if Matt is married or not, I am dry heaving. My mind keeps saying 'Surface now. See Matt.' Yet I cannot open the door. I need out. Only papa has the key. Mommy cannot even touch it. One day it will be passed to me and not even my spouse could touch it. It is one of the ruler-only items. After I feel the hour pass, making it twenty hours in here, I start screaming. Papa has not come yet. My body is not even hungry an hour after my normal mealtimes, so I know I have missed three meals before papa unlocks the door. As soon as he steps aside, I run pass him and up the stairs as fast as I can.

I fall often but get right back up and run. I pass Janice at the top of the stairs, but I do not stop running. I had to get to the surface. Had to see Matt. I hear Janice say, "You would think our border fish had been tormenting her with the way she acts, Meera."

Mom says, "Most do Janice. They have nothing in the cages except their thoughts. People do not handle being alone with their thoughts well. I thought Ann would have been better off as she was just doing a greatly reduced trade for someone else."

As I have fallen, again, they have caught up to me. Janice says, "Need the nourishment mix Ann."

I am running still. I fall again. I put up a scale shield as they get close again. I know if they touch me, they will learn about Matt. It would take hours to explain. I need to know if he is single. I need that information now. My body aches. My heart feels as if I am ripping it apart. At this point, I would gladly eat a pear just to get to see Matt and his smile. I would gladly eat twelve if he is single. If he is taken, I will have to tell him goodbye and never see him again. Meme walks through my shield, lowering it. Only guardians could lower my shield. Papa could if we were the same gender. Mom cannot as she does not rule.

Meme picks me up saying, "Nourishment mix Janice."

Janice tosses it to her saying, "Yes Guardian. What happened to Ann that she runs?"

Meme asks, "Need something Ann?"

I say, "Martha."

Minutes later, Martha comes over. She says, "Chris told me that if I could not get someone off my mind, chances are they called for me to visit them. Did you call to me Ann?"

She stays back the proper distance from Meme. I reach toward Martha, knowing she might understand. Meme orders her to come. Martha is arm length away. Meme lets me go understanding I was not sharing with most. My body has not processed the nourishment mix yet. I drop. Martha touches me. I open the knowledge flow to her, make her promise not to share with anyone then ask how she felt when Chris offered her the coral each time.

Martha replies she was stunned and confused with the gesture the first time, pleased and excited the second time. I ask about when she was down to three and I mentioned how close she was to marrying while the false document had not been voided. Martha tells me it felt as if her heart was being ripped apart because she wanted her Chris but was bound to her attacker. I ask about what that feeling told her. Martha states, "It is then I realized I was coming to love Chris. Is your heart aching Ann?"

I release her saying, "Thank you for the information. Remember you promised not to share with anyone."

Standing up now that my body has absorbed the nourishment mix, I run to the edge of the city. Then I swim. Once pass our boundaries I go up fast. Two hours later, I surface near the dense forest. I walk through it as Matt had mentioned not to run. The tigers hunted that way. Halfway through I drop to my knees. So drained. I still try to get to Matt. I must know if he is taken or we could possibility have a chance of a future together. Especially after Martha having told me, I was falling in love with him. I must know.

CHAPTER TWENTY-SEVEN

Good Information

A tiger comes over. It smells the air then its tung moves over its mouth. I recognize a hunger movement. I move back. Another tiger comes out of the forest and smacks the first one growling. The first one drops its head. The second tiger comes over to me faster then I can move away. It pushes its head under my right arm. Now I am hugging it. It growls slightly and the other tiger soon has my left arm around it. I do not even have the energy to see what they intend to do, let alone help or fight. I should have taken time to heal better before coming to the land.

Together the two tigers drag me to the pear tree. There they remove themselves from under my arms. Then they stand there roaring loudly. There is a commotion in the town. Minutes later, Matt comes over. He has some other people dump meat near the trees then Matt picks me up and carries me into the city. The other people follow him. As he walks, he asks, "What happened Ann?"

I reply, "Food."

Matt sits me in a chair at a table. He walks off. That causes me pain. Two minutes later, he sits a plate of dry people's food in front of me. I pick up the pear first and eat that. At least I know I can handle that. After that I say, "I have questions Matt. That is why I came to see you without even eating first."

To that Matt says, "Eat first. Then we can talk about whatever you want."

After I finish a few more bites, I ask, "Are you taken?"

Matt replies, "No. Interested in me?"

I state, "I am not going to allow myself to get more interested if you were taken. There would be no point, only useless pain."

Matt says, "Agreed. What other questions do you have?"

I move topic to the tigers' actions. He explains they were making sure the town would know something was wrong by getting me there and roaring. I keep our conversation light, just occasionally asking about him and telling him some about me. After my time nears an end, I go home.

CHAPTER TWENTY-EIGHT

Wedding

Two years pass this way, with me seeing Matt every other day and exploring the days I do not visit him. I am fully in love with Matt. I know seeing him marry another, or even finding out that he had would hurt me so bad I would be under Janice's care for months. Today is my eighteenth birthday. I stayed in the nation until after lunch so my parents could throw me the party as usual. Then I came to the outsider town where Matt lives. I wonder around looking for him without asking for him. I do not want to seem over eager.

None of the town here talks to me unless I talk to them or Matt is with me. Not that it matters, I have nothing to say to them and no reason to trust them. I think Matt is a nonmagic. Maybe I can convince him magics can be trusted. It might take a bit though. He is worth it. I want him my lifetime if he wants me. All three thousand or so years, if I live that long.

Fifteen minutes later, Matt comes over to me. He says, "Hi Ann. Wow you look nice. Why are you dressed up?"

I say, "My parents asked me to. It is normal as today is my birthday. I am eighteen."

Matt says, "Happy birthday. If I had known I would have got you a gift. I did want to invite you to dinner, but if you are expected back, it will have to wait."

I say, "My party was this morning. Dinner sounds good."

Matt says, "How about meeting my parents?"

Is he wanting to advance our friendship? Is this what Martha would call a date? Could I afford to date him when I love him already? Could I not date him loving him so much? I know I must look stunned. I smile saying, "I want to meet them. They must be nice people to raise someone nice."

Matt asks, "You care for me?"

I reply, "You are nice."

Matt laughs, takes my hand and walks off. I let him lead me. Matt asks, "Are you fine with my being a royal?"

Is he a royal? Is he fine with my being a royal? I ask, "Are you?"

Matt replies, "I am the prince of this nation. Are you fine with that?"

I reply, "It is fine. What is for dinner?"

Matt says, "I know you enjoy eating fish, so I have boiled lobster planned. Plus, since it is your birthday, I will have the chef make cake for dessert."

I ask, "What is cake?"

Matt says, "Your culture is deprived."

I repeat my question, "What is cake?"

Matt replies, "A sweet bread type of food."

I say, "I do not try bread. Simply not interested."

Matt says, "You do not try many things. What are some of your birthday traditions to eat?"

I reply, "Fish is a special treat where I live."

Matt asks, "What is everyday food then?"

I reply, "Seaweed, kelp, algae."

Matt asks, "Do you enjoy it?"

I reply, "Yes. I grew up on it."

We reach the castle gates then. The guards let us through, me after Matt had told them I was his guest. We go to the throne room. There I see the king I had met. He says, "Ann, good to see you. I did not expect to see you here."

I say, "Kind sir. I take it Matt is your son."

He replies, "Yes. I am Henry and this is my wife Diana."

I say, "Lady Queen."

Diana says, "Call me Diana please."

We sit down and eat boiled lobster, lettuce which I think is somewhat similar to kelp, and shrimp with a round thing. I hold that up asking, "What is this?"

Matt replies, "A bun. One style of bread."

I place it on his plate taking all the shrimp off of it in one swift movement. Matt laughs, "Not even going to try it?"

To that I ask, "What is yeast?"

Matt says, "It makes bread increase in size, so we get more out of it."

I ask, "What is it? You told me what it does, but not what it is."

Matt says, "I do not really know."

I ask, "Yet you eat it? Not me."

Matt says, "Grew up with it. It is good."

I say, "Well bread and things similar to it is something we can agree that you can have all you want of them."

Matt says, "Want to dance Ann?"

Since my outfit has long gloves as part of it and he holds out his hand, I reply, "What is dance?"

Henry says, "Deprived culture."

I say, "Yours is strange to me to. What is dance?"

Matt says, "Lead you through it."

He does. It reminds me of the fish jibes. I mention that then Matt and his parents ask to see one. I focus on Matt only then on the fish jibes. In moments I am in movement. When I stop Matt says, "You dance really well."

I say, "I did not know what you meant by dance, but I do fish jibes decently well."

We dance to music for a bit before Matt somewhat kneels before me, confusing me. He pulls out a small box and opens it to reveal a stunning ring. Matt asks, "Marry me Ann?"

Shock causes me to gasp. I had not expected him to ask, let alone on my birthday. It is the best gift ever. I know my parents, their council (if united in the decision) or worse the guardians of the land could remove my magic and would if they thought that I had become a danger to the safety of the nation. If the guardians removed my magic, I would have no chance of getting it back. I know that I might lose my birthright and the friends I had grown up with, just to be with him. I accept the risks as I love him that much, I hurt being away from him. Knowing Warrior would attack him first and ask questions later, I accept asking, "Might I have a month to let my parents know and do some wedding preparation, I will be back after that to be your wife and will live here with you. I love you."

I would end up hurt too as I would protect my Matt. He wants me! I feel light as a jellyfish now. When I did not know if he was involved but was getting interested in him, I felt as a great white shark. His proposal makes me so happy and I feel so good. This yummy man wants me as I want him. Um yum. If I thought I could have time to explain while Matt and his parents were with me, I would take them all to my home now. However, warrior will not even give outsiders a chance. I am not sure what he holds against them. I cannot put them in danger. It must wait. Especially as no one knows of my surface trips or that I have been seeing anyone.

Matt says, "I do not have any problem with that, my Ann. See you in a month."

Henry and Diana say, "It is good to let your family know you want to be married. Love to meet them if they are able to come visit."

I give Matt a quick hug and walk out. As I walk through the forest back to the river, I hide my ring. No mer will see it until after I tell my parents and their council. I know the guardians will know as soon as I touch the water, but I can keep it from everyone else. My parents should be the first to know. Telling the council at the same time is faster and easier then repeating myself. That way they can all decide as a unit if I remain a mer or if I lose everything that I grew up with for Matt. I love the sea and its life, I truly do. I just cannot give up my Matt. It hurts too much to be away from him.

When I touch the water, at sunset, Meme says, "Your parents and people are worried child."

I dive as I reply, "I expect so. It has been longer than I usually do."

Meme asks, "Mind telling me why you decided to stay on the land so long?"

I reply, "Lost tract of time."

Meme asks, "Doing what?"

I answer, "Fish jibes. They call it dancing. I danced with my..."

My voice trailed off. I feel myself blushing. Meme asks, "Your love? You are married now?"

I state, "Not yet. Engaged though. I want the sea and its ways, but I need him."

Meme says, "No mer has ever gave up the one they love. Of course, mers mostly choose other mers to be with. You have always been different. You explore further. You interact with more people. You even test our limits. Does your love take care of you when you are with him?"

I say, "I get fish often. Though he does not have right to get them from the sea, I do. I do not mind the cost incurred to keep him safe. He does not know. His people only grab what they will eat now. At least the ones I interact with. They all know I am his friend and have a strict standard on not taking more than needed."

Meme asks, "You still want mer life?"

I nod. Then I place my canteens in my thinking place, talk to Tark for a moment before going the rest of the way home. On entering the mer boundaries, I feel the stress I put everyone under. For that I am terribly sorry. Then my parents' knowledge flow is open. They ask, "Why were you gone so long today Ann?"

Also using magic, I reply, "I had dinner with a friend. I am sorry to worry you."

The flow closes. I know they accepted my answer. I swim right to the gathering room were the throne is located. I sit down outside and wait for the scheduled council meeting three days from now. I will talk with them all at once after their normal meeting. The only difference in this meeting than over the last four years, on a monthly basis is that I will not be a part of it. It would not be right to attend the meeting without magic. Since I do not know what they will decide, I cannot attend the meeting.

Two days later, as the council came one at a time they say, "Ann you can join us if you want to."

I reply to each of them, "I ask to talk to you all when the meeting is over. I will wait until the meeting is over."

My parents had invited me into the meeting as well, but I had begged to be allowed to stay here until after the meeting. I wanted to talk to them all. Their important meeting should be first. My parents reluctantly agreed. After the meeting they have me come in. Papa asks, "What is so important that you would wait until we were all together, Ann?"

They all want to know. While I usually call them father, mother, and friends, as they are the closest to friends I have here, I say, "Sire king, madam queen and honored council."

Though I see their confusion on that, I cannot stop, or they would get sidetracked from the main issue. I do not even pause before stating, "I am engaged, and I plan to live with him in his land."

Then I ask them to decide if I kept my magic or not, as either way, I intended to marry him. That causes mass confusion as no one had even realized I had been seeing anyone and did not even know that I had any guy friends. The council and their heirs not included. My only true friend in the mer nation was Martha. They all know they had lost contact with me every day for an hour to four and so know that the man I love was not a Mer. If the one I love was a mer they would had known I was interested in someone and marriage as that one would have asked my father for permission to ask for my agreement to be his wife. They all say, "Must be a nonmagic. When did you first go above the water?"

I reply, "I brought Martha here about two months after I first crossed the surface. I swim as they do, move the way they do and nearly talk the way they do. They just assume I live in a costal town. I say my home is near the water. You cannot get any nearer to the water then in it. They know my culture is different but that is expected as I do not live in their area. They even have different cultures and ways of talking among themselves. It took me a bit to learn enough to communicate with them where they learned nothing of this place. Wela and Martha helped me learn it faster. Would you all please decide on if I stay a part of the sea life now."

Equal parts thought it was unsafe as thought it could be safe. The council was talking all at once. Telling each other their opinion and the reasons they held that opinion. Though they are all talking my magic understands everything said. I learned that warrior has a high disdain for outsiders as his sister was put into a cage when they were young and after a few years she gave him all mer related items so the dry people did not get hold of them and killed herself a few days later. They had hurt her so much she stopped wanting to live. My whole-body aches for the children they were and what they lost then. I ask what all she experienced to lead her to thinking death was better then anything when we all hold life as the most precious treasure there is.

Warrior shows her getting caught in a net, struggling to get free. Changing to human as they pulled her onto their boat. Her passing out from the pain of holding her air. All the cuts down her body from the net. Her not understanding anything they said. Them giving her a bath, but she was too weak to keep human appearances, so she ended up in a glass cage for everyone to stare at. Him having to act as one of the humans so to get close to her yet warn her to act as if she feared him too without letting the humans catch on. Three years trying to escape to fail daily. Her finally begging him to take her mer items home and declare her dead. His saying he could not lie to everyone. She told him it would not be a lie as she was not going to continue living as a captive. She then killed herself in front of him.

I feel tears on my face. I look around. The entire council is crying. We all understand his pain on seeing his sister take her life. It felt as if a swordfish had pierced my heart. Still I know not all nonmagics are that way. My Matt and his parents are far better than that. Some could easily be persuaded either direction but if I go there, I can influence them stronger to help the world then if I stay here. I remind everyone I still need their answer if I remained their princess, or even a mer. It is soon calm emotions as they all nod then back to trying to decide if I should still be a mer, let alone their princess. They all care what happens to me, yet they do not seem to be able to agree if my remaining a mer is best for everyone.

Meme and some of her equals show up. Instant quiet. We all wait for their decision on my magic and right to rule after papa. I want the sea, but I need my Matt. My eyes water as I figure I will lose my home. Their decision is final. No one opposes it no matter what they have decided. I will never be allowed back if they tell me to give up my magic for him. I would do so. I just do not wish to. Meme says, "Ann be incredibly careful about using your magic around others and you will need to return here to the Mer nation at least once a year. Doing so will give you strength and assure the people that you are safe, therefor that they are safe. We will allow the marriage and you will be queen here. Take your place as queen."

What? I am so confused. I thought I had lost everything here for Matt. Not only did I not lose my home I now rule it. I walk over to papa dazed. I say, "Love you Papa. You made me strong."

Papa replies, "My Queen, it was right to make sure you could rule."

I grip my mom in a hug saying, "Thank you for always showing me your love mom. It made me brave enough to chase my own."

Mom says, "Of course, dear. You needed our love, so you knew how it looked and to never settle for less. Such as your friend Martha went through."

I say, "Martha. She helped me learn by showing me different words, speaking those words and showing me the images that they meant. Plus, though she knows a deep pain she also loves deeply. I intend to ask her to care for my baby when I have one. That way the nation's heir grows up in the nation. I know you will all help my child learn to be a good ruler for the people, just as you helped me. Everything I learned from you all made me strong enough and brave enough to go to the surface. Now I can teach the dry people to care about the world. I will start with my Matt. He already cares some. It is my magic he does not know about."

Meme asks, "Why not?"

I reply, "Outsider. You warned me even today to be careful of my magic around them. I do not know if I could ever tell him because if he rejects me for it, I think I could not handle that. I want all my life as his wife. If I live the five thousand years some mers have, I would want my Matt to be with me through it all. Yet I do not know how to tell him. I know I cannot this year. I want to so there are no secrets between us, but until we are married, I cannot be alone with him enough to mention it without others learning it as well. I know it could be grounds for the deception clause and could void our union if he decided that, but I cannot think of any other way. I hope he accepts me still when I can tell him."

Warrior asks, "Why not on your wedding night then?"

I ask, "Would you be able to mention life altering information on a special day?"

Warrior says, "Probably not. Then again, I do not have the risk you have as I only want a mer and will live all my life alone until I find her."

Janice asks, "Is this Matt why you ran out of the cages?"

I say, "I could not get him off my mind and I did not know if he was taken. I had to know. I ran as soon as I could then swam to the surface before running to find him and learn it. I knew if you touched me when I was so needy of information, you would know I was interested in someone and ask questions I was not ready to answer as I did not know the answers myself. It was not until Martha shared about her feelings on her Chris proposing to her twice, and her running on the group rotations that I understood I cared about Matt. I was starting to love him. I made her promise not to share about our discussion so I could learn if he were taken before I subjected myself to many questions."

Builder asks, "How did you meet this Matt?"

I reply, "I had gotten lost while exploring. He helped me find my way back to the river. I walked down its edges until I was unseen and alone before I swam home. That was only a bit after I had met Martha. I was attracted to him from the start, but I dismissed it as his treating me as a friend while I did not have friends here. Do not try saying otherwise. No one would try to outrace me. They always treated me as their princess first. I understand it now, but I did not understand it when I was in school. My loneliness made me explore. Finding Matt seemed to calm that. I mean I still explore but the area is always near where he is. I met him in the town where he lives every other day. We stayed in the town walking around and talking. Others followed us. I learned recently they are his father's warriors. I wondered why they would until I learned on my eighteenth birthday that he is the prince there. I never asked as according to mer laws, others had to be with us. It is just that it was different then most there and I wondered about it. I do not ask if I am not sure how to safely do so. Matt made sure I was taken care of. The fish Wela showed everyone, that was an image I had showed her. I bought the debt from the outsiders as Matt was there. Matt and I gave the fish to some animals that live near that town. Most outsiders are afraid of those animals. I do not know why. What was not shown was that I had touched the display the fish were in to see if they had been purchased from us. I was told not to touch the glass. The dry person insulted Matt so he touched the display many times before paying for the fish, only the fish and refusing to pay for the cleaning of the display before we walked out. I should have guessed Matt was of importance in the town then, but I was focused on learning what an animal was. Now that I am calm again, the people should know the changes."

The council nods. The doors are opened and the council orders everyone to come into the room. Soon everyone has taken their normal seats. While at meals some face away from the throne, interacting with their own clans or families, now is different. This is a national order call. Everyone faces the throne. The council is standing in front of my parents and me. They hide the change from the people, letting everyone get seated first. It is quiet as the order call says it is important. Once everyone is seated, the council takes their seats. There is an explosion of noise as all mers question why I am on the throne, holding the ruling items and wearing the crown not my father. Papa orders quiet, but no one listens as they are confused. Nodding at each other my parents go sit at the single table I use to. At that I realize rule has fully passed to me. I hit the rod of the ruler's staff against the floor briefly. The last command everyone heard is soon obeyed as I had done so. It is once again quiet.

The council stands. Warrior says, "Everyone can tell that Ann is now Queen. Her parents have stepped down. We called the meeting as Queen Ann has something to say to everyone."

Facing me he says, "My Queen."

The council sits as I stand. I say, "I love being a mer. I love our good sea. However, in my exploring beyond our boundaries, I met some outsiders. I brought Martha here as she needed to get away from the surface people that live on the dry land. Her pain I cannot share with you. Yet even after seeing it, I still explored the land. I met other dry people. I fell in love with one of them. He loves me. We will be married. The guardians already gave me their approval. I will be gone often, a lot, but I will return once a year. Your safety has always been and will always be of concern to me. I will protect you from any threat, even if it hurts me. Long live the mer nation!"

My people call back, "Long live the mer nation! Long live Queen Ann!"

They chant it. I walk out. I go to my room here and get some rest. When I wake up, I go to the library. Our books are not as dry people's books. Dry people use something called paper, made from trees Martha has told me. I do not understand how, and she is not sure of the process. Mer books are recorded messages into seashells. There are many in here. I place my staff and all related ruling items except the ring and matching bracelet in their spaces knowing I could not take them with me, and no magic would touch them. They know better. Water magics would suffocate. Fire or neutral magics would drown. Non magics if they managed to get this far would drown. Only myself or my descendants could safely move them or even touch them. I cannot take them with me as they are magic identifiers.

Done with that, I slowly go to the surface, so my people have time to adjust to my energy leaving them now that I rule. They do not need to go into shock from the sudden energy loss. Once I reach the shore, I lower my ability to hear my people, so their energy stays strong. I walk upriver, walking in the water and crawling pass the houses. Two weeks later, I see an injured girl about my age. Safe or not, I can heal her. It will take a bit of energy from my people, but it would be wrong to let her suffer when I can help. I go over to her. Somehow, I trust her without a doubt of my safety near her. I say, "Hi. I am Merth Ann. I am a mermaid healer. Let me help you."

She nods saying, "Mermaid has nothing to fear from me. I am crystal magic."

I heal her. She then says, "Thank you; I know that you risked your safety to help me so if you ever need my help just say my name 'Orval' and rub this crystal. I will come."

Thinking she wants to repay me and probably would not accept my refusal I put the small crystal into a pocket, next to where I had put the mer ruler's bracelet and ring. The ring is authority over the mer. The bracelet is absolute control over the mers, not including guardian rank. I would need to pass them to my descendant, so if anything happened to me before the baby was three days old, that one could rule the mers. Orval and I go our separate ways. A week later, I arrive in the city around where Matt lives, right on time. Matt is excited to see me. I am equally excited to see him. Diana says, "Do you have anything picked out for your wedding dress Ann?"

I reply, "I am open to suggestions."

Diana leads me to a dress shop. I say, "Diana, I do not have the currency used here."

She scuffs, "You are about to be family. Do not worry about it."

I drop my head in acceptance of her words. Diana says, "You are used to paying for things are you not?"

Smiling I say, "I have even taken on other's debt to make their lives easier. It is strange for me to allow others to buy for me."

Diana says, "You can consider it a wedding gift."

If she keeps up, I will be in tears before too long. My people would feel that. I say, "Alright. What dress do you think your son would enjoy seeing on me the most?"

Diana replies, "Honestly, none. He is looking forward to having you as his."

I turn bright red muttering, "Not the only one. Move on please."

Diana says, "Glad you feel that way. Let us see, something low cut to give him a glimpse of what he has to look forward to but not so low most would see."

I follow her down row after row of dresses. She shoves aside many I would have tried on. However, as I want to look perfect for my Matt, I just follow and trust his mother's opinion.

An hour later, we have barely walked a third of the store. She has rejected most of the dresses. I am tired of this. Still I want to look absolutely stunning for Matt, and I hope he will not take his eyes off of me, so I continue on.

Another two hours and we have finished the store. She has picked out seven dresses for me to try on. They all seem either to low cut on top to suit me or to high cut on the slit up the bottom to suit me. I decide I would rather show a bit of leg then my chest, so I grab one of those three and go try it on. Nope! Will not do. It shows half of my mer marking. I grab the seams and move my hand down until the mark is hidden. It takes half of the slit away. I put a clamp I made out of one of my scales over that area and walk out to show Diana.

Diana asks, "You do not care for the dress?"

I say, "This is as high as I will wear any slit. Not any higher. Nothing can convince me otherwise."

Diana says, "Alright."

Then she removes both of the other dresses that had slits, tosses me one of the four with a low-cut top and tells me to try it on. I go do so. No way! Seriously no way! It shows the royalty mark of the mer nation. To low. To hide that mark I would have to wear a shirt underneath this dress. I take it off, put back on the outfit I wore here then walk out. I say, "No offense Diana, but I do not want anything that low either."

Diana says, "You enjoy making things difficult, do you?"

I say, "No. I just have strong opinions on how much I am willing to show anyone besides Matt and only after law says we are married, and we are alone."

Diana says, "Well let us look again."

I say, "You look. I wait here."

She walks off as I sit down. I need to hide my marks. It is actually one mark that wraps around my upper right thigh crosses my back and covers my upper chest. In it is all laws of the mer nation, the national boundaries, and restricted royal only names for the mer people. It also tells that to get immortality one had to be accepted by the ancients and by the stars. The top has my full name placed in it along with my rank. It changed automatically as my rank changed. The bottom states that I am part of the mer nation. No way would I let anyone see that mark or any part of it. I am not ready to share.

Diana comes back with three dresses. She hands me one. I try to try it on, but the arms are to small. My arms are slender but not that tiny. After I tell Diana that, she hands me another dress. I cannot zip it up. I tell Diana that. She hands me the last dress. It fits. I do not care all that much for the wide-open stomach area, but it hides all my mark. This is it then. I hope Matt enjoys what I go through for him. I go out and show Diana. She asks, "Do you care for that one?"

I say, "Better then the others you picked out that I could actually fit into."

Diana says, "Matt will love seeing you in it."

I say, "Matt would love seeing me **out of it** later that evening."

We laugh. Diana states, "I am sure he will. Get changed into the outfit you wore here and let me pay for your dress."

I change. She pays for it. I follow her from place to place getting things, ordering other things and sampling still other things. When she comes to the bakery, I say, "I do not do bread or cakes."

Diana says, "However, most people do. This will be a national holiday after all. Everyone will be here. All of our people, and a good deal many of our allies. You enjoy cake or not is your choice. It will be offered to the guests."

I say, "Sure. They can have as much as they want. Just as long as I do not have to eat anything I do not want to."

After all the blah planning is done, I am shown to a room in the castle and told it would be guarded so Matt and I were not together before our marriage. Yea whatever. I go in closing the door behind me and ask Meme to suppress my mer marking. I needed it to be hidden for a year. That would give me time to adjust to not being in the water so much. I fall asleep with no response. I wake up without a trace of my mer mark. I feel drained. I join Henry and Diana for breakfast. Diana says, "Matt is having breakfast in his quarters. He asked not to see you until he could take you there without issues as he has no control left not to if he sees you. His words."

I blush deeply. Wow, I so do not need that this early. I eat then ask, "Is there a pool in the castle? I enjoy swimming."

Diana leads me to the pool room. I dive forcing myself to keep human appearances. I open the knowledge flow to all my people asking if anyone needed anything. Nothing for most. A small child of five lets only me know that she wants a sister. I tell her to let her parents know. They might have a second child, but I could not guarantee that happening, let alone the gender if it did occur. Then I remind her it is a rare occurrence. She nodded. The knowledge flow had to end as they were getting tired.

At dinner I am escorted to the meal then to my room here until my marriage. A week passes by this way. Then Diana comes early asking, "Ready to be married to Matt yet?"

I reply, "Been ready since he proposed."

Diana says, "We love you too Ann. After breakfast you will be brought back here to change into your dress. Just a bit later then our normal lunchtime is the ceremony. Are your parents going to be here?"

I say, "I had not asked them to be."

Diana asks, "You do not want them here?"

I say, "Different culture. They would feel as if they had to try things served to eat to not be rude. To much they do not know. Remember I asked many questions even when Matt proposed a month ago."

Diana says, "An ally of ours will be marrying you to Matt. Since you are eighteen your parents do not have to give their approval. I will lead you down to him."

I smile. We go to breakfast. I eat as fast as I can, what I can with my excitement shutting my appetite off. Then Diana has a guard escort me back to the room I am using, so I can change. I pack up the few items I own and hand it to a female servant telling her to bring it to me after Matt and I were married, that I would know if she tried to open it and that it was rigged to hurt whoever tried to open it without the code. I do not mention it is mer sealed. Only a fish person could open it. The servant girl nods and walks off. I was wrapped in a thick blanket when talking to her and she was the only one in the room.

Now I get into the dress. This is lovely. Not caring for the dress still, but I am so excited to be getting married to Matt. He will officially be mine after today. I contact my parents asking them if they wanted to be at my wedding. They do not as though they approve of how happy he makes me; they do not fully trust the dry people to have all living mer royals in one area not in the mer nation. They tell me they love me and made something for my wedding. They show me an image of each of them taking a scale off, forging the scales together and making me a hair clip. It is fancy and I find I want to wear it now. I ask them to have Meme get an equal to deliver it to me if she would. Then I close the knowledge flow.

Just before normal lunch time here Diana joins me. She asks, "Excited?"

I say, "That is among the many emotions I am experiencing. Do you really think Matt will enjoy seeing me in this dress?"

Diana says, "Sweety, my son loves you. He will enjoy whatever you wear, especially nothing."

I say, "OK. Enough. I am already warm enough. Your people want to actually see the ceremony."

Diana laughs. Then taking my hand she says, "This way dear, to become part of our family."

I follow her saying, "You are just part of the deal I get with my Matt."

Diana laughs again. Then she asks, "How long have you loved him?"

I reply, "From the time I first met him even though I did not know his name. He treated me as a friend when not even the people of the city I called home did. Combined with his looks, I was obsessed."

Diana laughs, "Over two years?"

I say, "I think so."

Then we are outside. I see Matt at the end of a long walkway. My Matt. I want to run to him, but my feet seem to heavy to manage more then walking. It seems to take me hours to walk the distance though it is only minutes. Matt looks at me full of desire. I do not remember what occurs next until I am pronounced to be Matt's wife. His kiss I have nothing to compare to. When he releases me someone I have never met comes up. This woman says, "Pardon. Someone called Meme asked me to deliver this to you. She said your parents had asked her to get it to you for your wedding."

I glance at her wondering about her words then take the small box. Opening it I see the headband my parents had shown me they made for my wedding. I squeal. As I put it on Matt asks, "Why does that make you so happy?"

Laughing, I reply, "It is only made to order by the parents of the woman getting married where I am from. Both parents have to give the order and approve of the union. This head band is the ultimate gift I could get from them and is exceedingly rare in the town I am from. It means both of my parents are happy for us."

Matt says, "Alright. What is the other thing in the box?"

I ask, "Other thing?"

Looking I squeal again. I take it out and say, "Oh wow they did. Matt this is for you. It means they accept you into their family. Also, an exceedingly rare item they would both have to agree on to order."

Matt says, "If it is something that makes you happy, I will wear it."

He puts it on. Diana says, "Henry and I are glad you are part of our family now Ann."

Henry says, "Welcome to the family Ann."

I thank them. Matt and I open the rest of the gifts. Then we thank everyone for coming again and go sit down waiting for dinner to be served. Minutes later, food is served to everyone. I notice a huge selection of fish and wonder if the sea cleared the fish for release. I say, "Fish please."

The cart is brought over to me. I see simple words that translate to, "We send these to wherever our Queen Ann lives now for her wedding. The mer council."

I smile and take as much as I can eat. This is the best they could give me. After the meal is dancing. I ask low for Matt to lead me through the dances because if I did fish jibes, I might make them question if I am suited to be his. Matt agrees to do so saying they really had no say and it was past their control now. I know but I do not want to do the fish mating dance for anyone except him and there are two many people here. The dancing lasts until dinner time when we all eat again. After dinner Matt takes me into the castle. The servant girl I talked to earlier brings me over my things, still bagged up. Her hands appear to be swordfish cut though. I say, "I warned you not to try to open my bag. Had you asked, I might have shown you some of what is so special to me. As it is, you should get away from me or anyone that know me and stay away as I will attack you and so will those who know me. The only reason I give you this warning is because Matt makes me to happy to directly punish you for tampering with my stuff. Get lost!"

She gasps, "Yes Princess."

Then she runs off dropping my bag. Matt leads me into his room. It is our room now. I feel my magic place a barrier around the room then feel that barrier move through me as we enter the room. I sleep in the next morning. Seeing me awake, Matt says, "Good morning, beautiful. It is almost lunch time. Did I exhaust you that much?"

I blush deeply then mutter, "I dehydrate easily remember. Until my body even out I sleep. It was wow though."

Matt laughs. We join his parents for lunch. Diana's grin makes my face heat up. I decide to focus on food. My magic tells me something has changed. After I eat, I go for a swim. It feels so good to be in the water. Sleeping in the mer nation, even if in the water is normal. I am so tired; I nearly forget the dry people do not sleep near water. I get out and go back to Matt and my room. I wake up for breakfast the next day. Matt asks, "Still dehydrated love?"

I reply, "Slightly."

Matt asks, "Yet you do not drink more water?"

I say, "I have learned to not jump extremes. I get sick. That only dehydrates me more."

Matt says, "Alright, please hydrate enough where you do not sleep so much. It concerns me."

I say, "Going for a swim."

CHAPTER TWENTY-NINE

Learning and Sharing of Magic

Matt walks with me. Today there is no one else in the pool. It would be a good time to tell Matt of my magic, but I am scared of his rejection. We just swim together for a bit, until my energy drops so much, he has to carry me back to our room. I sleep until lunch the next day. Matt refuses to let me swim after my meal thinking it exhausts me faster. He does not realize it helps me hydrate as he does not know of my magic. It takes me three days to wake up. Matt asks, "What happened Ann?"

I reply, "Told you I dehydrate fast. Swimming slows my need for water. I was raised in a town near the sea. Matt, I need water to stay awake. So tired."

Matt brings me a glass of water from our bathroom. I drink it then say, "Fill the tub and join me for a bath Matt."

He whispers some romantic things to me causing me to blush. Matt then says, "I do not think you are up to it though so I will let you get some more rest. Join my parents and me for whatever meal when you are rehydrated sweetheart."

I kiss him before letting him leave. Once the door closes, I sigh. I had gotten enough courage to tell him and he left the room over joining me. I go take a bath crying. At this rate, we might go years before he learns of my magic. I do not undress as my magic manipulates over the material to form my tail. I do not use soap as the water is what

I need. Soap would dry out my scales. I close my eyes and relax, having locked the bathroom door. As I relax my body changes into my mer form. I ask, "Meme, why has my magic flows altered?"

Meme says, "Usually happens with a child. Are you pregnant?"

I reply, "How soon would I know for sure?"

Meme replies, "About a week along. However, outsiders do not know for four months. You could not mention it until then if you are. Also, they carry nine months so your body would have to match that for the outsiders to accept that your husband is your child's father. We know it could only be him as no one else would live, but outsiders do not know that, and you could not safely explain it to them. Are you pregnant?"

I say, "Bit to soon to know. Matt and I have only been married for a few days."

Just then I hear the bathroom door handle rattle, so I quickly say bye to Meme and end the connection, change back to my human appearance and ask who it is. It is my Matt, so I unlock the door. Matt says, "I changed my mind and thought I would join you. Why are you taking a bath fully dressed?"

I reply, "Just decided to."

Somehow, I lost the courage that I had mere minutes ago to tell him of my magic. He sits on the tub edge asking, "Is the offer to join you still good?"

I look away. If he doubts it then I have no business wanting him to. Matt says, "Sure. Whatever. Enjoy your bath."

He stands up and I yank him into the water, changing to my mer form and placing myself over him as I do. Matt gasps in shock, struggles to the surface, pushing me to the side. He holds me out of the way, not looking at me as he yells. I do not hear most of it as I am upset that he is yelling at me and pushing me. I do hear the words crazy and stupid in the mix.

Fine. Matt no longer wants me then I will solve the problem for him. I change back to human looks, get out of the tub, go over to my wash bag, take out a sea urchin, and with my mer magic I command it to completely dry me out. It objects reminding me that such would hurt or kill me. I know, yet if Matt does not want me mere days after our marriage then I have nothing to live for. I repeat my command. It sighs and starts drying my arm. In moments, my arm is pealing skin and feels numb. The urchin moves spots. That area is numb and pealing in moments. When it moves again, Matt forcefully pulls it off and tosses it into the tub then tries to drag me out of the room. I struggle saying, "Let go. You want me gone. I will give you that."

Matt says, "I do not want you gone, you crazy girl. I want you to think about what you do. I could have drowned. The action you did was stupid. Do you want me gone?"

I say, "Why are you insulting me? Let me go. Just let me die. You do not trust me; I have no reason left to live."

Matt kisses me passionately. Yum. I relax. My Matt still loves me. I wrap my arms around him unable to do anything else. Matt pulls me closer. I lean into him. Matt relaxes his grip asking, "Still want to die Ann?"

I say, "I never did. I just did not want to live without you."

Matt asks, "So what reason do you have for trying to end my life?"

I say, "Matt, I just wanted you to join me. To be with me. I did not want to sound as if I was begging you to love me."

Matt says, "I prefer you to slightly beg me to be with you over scaring me that you want me dead."

I say, "I love you Matt. I would never intentionally do anything to hurt you. I love you and I want you."

Matt says, "I want you too. How do you feel about trying for children?"

I reply with a blush, "Give."

A few days later, my mer magic lets me know I am for sure pregnant. I am so, so happy. Matt and I are expanding our family. A week later, I start having mild pain. I think nothing of it. I do not even think anything of it when my pain increases as Matt gets close to me. I decide to surprise Matt on his birthday a few months from now with news of my being pregnant. However, after three months in pain and more then the stories left from my ancestors, with it increasing when Matt gets near me, I start trying to avoid him to avoid the pain. I do not know what I am going to do on his birthday. How will I stand the pain?

I manage to avoid Matt completely for two weeks before he corners me asking, "Ann why do you avoid me? Do you regret marrying me? If it would make you happy, you can leave. I hope you stay though."

Though in pain I still love him with everything I have. I reply, "I love you dearly and am happy to be your wife. I just don't feel very well."

Matt kisses me briefly before saying, "Alright Ann, get some rest and feel better soon. I love you."

I tell him I love him too. He leaves me alone. I wonder if I should go to my nation. The healers would be able to help me I am sure. However, Matt does not yet know of my magic so he cannot go there yet. Add to that once there, I will have to stay until after my twins are born, and my going there would feel as if I left Matt to him. I am certain it would. I do not wish to hurt him so. Yes, I did say twins. I feel two babies growing in me. Beautiful little girls. One reminds me some of Diana. The other one reminds me of the etchings done of my father's mother. She ruled before papa. Matt is going to be so excited when I tell him in fifteen days. Maybe after that, I should give a reason to visit my nation and be there for a long bit.

Over the next two weeks, the pain increases so much it hurts to move. I barely get around our quarters. I am near tears whenever Matt enters. I slightly curl up when he does trying to protect my babies and myself. Why does it hurt to be near him? Matt comes in today with his parents and another woman. This other woman wears things Madeline did, so I know she is a doctor. Having seen how they treat their patients I am not accepting that. I say, "No Matt. I will not allow a doctor near me. She leaves or I do. I will leave and stay away for months."

Matt asks, "Ann why will you not let the doctor near you? She is here to help you."

I reply, "I do not trust doctors. I won't let her near me."

Matt says, "Leave doc."

The doctor leaves. Matt's parents follow. Matt sits by me asking, "Why do you not trust doctors?"

I say, "I do not want to talk right now."

Then I yawn. Matt kisses my forehead as he leaves me alone. He is worried otherwise he would not have asked the doctor to come. I understand that. However, only healer Janice or her heir would I willingly allow near me. Only they would I know could help me.

Two months later, I am in so much pain I cannot even get up. Matt again has the doctor come. Again, his parents come in at the same time. I had totally slept through Matt's birthday and have yet to tell him I am pregnant. I do not need him worrying about our babies as well as me. I want to move away from the doctor as she comes close, but my body hurts too much to do so. As she sits by me to check me out, I say, "You may be able to check me out but you do not know my normal patterns so I am not going to accept anything you think of as treatment for me. You are just wasting your time. It is better spent helping someone that is willing to let you."

The doctor gets up goes over to Matt and his parents as they were standing by the door and says, "As long as Ann refuses treatment, there is nothing that I or anyone else could do. I am sorry young sire. She will not let me even try to help her."

Doctor leaves. Matt's parents follow. I am glad they stay out of my space for the most part. Matt looks sad. I realize he thinks I am going to die. All my ancestors recorded feeling very tired and only slight discomfort. I should be feeling the same. Why is it so different for me? Maybe Orval can help. I grab the crystal she handed me and call out to her. It is worth the try anyways. I cannot leave Matt and go to the mer nation yet, not to be there three months until my babies are born. Humans show when they are pregnant. Mers do not until the last month. Matt has no clue that is what is wrong, the reason I am in pain.

Matt comes over and sits by me, but I am focused on asking Orval for help. Seven minutes later, Orval comes in. She sees Matt so close to me and shoves him away. My pain decreases slightly, but I do not want my Matt hurt. Orval demands, "What did you do to her?!"

I say, "Orval, please do not hurt my husband."

Orval looked at me seeming surprised, then she faces Matt saying, "Sir, I apologize for shoving you. Please forgive me."

Facing me she asks, "Friend, do you realize that your husband is a fire type magic?"

What? Oh no! Our babies could die! They must be hurting each other. That explains the extreme pain. Matt could die from my guardians from the deception. I am just as bad and could die from his guardians. Oh, my family! Matt thinks I am human otherwise he would have said something long ago. I thought he was human. My family! Orval says, "You did not know."

Scared, confused and hurting, I ask, "Can you help me, Orval?"

Orval answers, "I don't know if I can. I will do my best however, and it could be painful, also I will have to take you away from everything you know."

Understanding, I know I have to let her try, so I say, "Please try."

Matt says, "Try please, I don't want to lose my Ann."

That calms me slightly as he trusts Orval. Her crystal magic is strong to get both of us to trust her on just meeting her. I relax slightly as she picks me up. I hear her mutter incredibly low, "Ethro follow."

I wonder what she meant. I close my eyes in a fit of pain. When I open my eyes, I am somewhere else. I do not know where. Looking around I see many crystals big enough to fit people inside them. Looking closer I realize they were made into homes. The pain I was feeling where I live with my Matt is almost gone here. It feels more as the recordings my ancestors left. This is normal mer pregnancy and I can deal with it. I smile saying, "Being here helps a lot and I am no longer in pain."

Orval says, "It is good you are not in pain. However, your husband would hate not seeing you for a while, you have to go back. The pain has a good chance of returning. Therefore, I am naming you my heir for your helping me when I needed it. You are now the crystal people's princess. Welcome to our world."

She is a queen? She did what? Her heir? Then I realize I am not even feeling any pain now. I am now Queen of the mers and a princess in two nations. With not feeling any pain, I wonder if my twins are alright. I feel my magic to learn what occurred. I am very shocked to feel four babies. Quads! No one has had quads before.

I feel their energy signatures as crystal people can apparently do that. One is a complete mer. She is the one that reminds me of grandma. As grandma was named Mertha, I will give her that name. One is completely fire energy. That is the one that reminds me of Diana. I will call her that. One is entirely a crystal and looks similar to Orval. Then there is one that looks similar to me but has Matt's red eyes. She has all three energies. I do not get how she lives. She and the little crystal girl stay between Mertha and Diana. I know they are keeping their sisters from hurting. I ask, "Orval, do you mind if I name one of my quads after you? I was thinking Orvalina."

Orval gets watery eyes as she says, "Oh the little princess has my name. I will not be forgotten."

I say, "Not just your name. She has your looks as well. I wanted to tell my Matt first about his twins, but I was in too much pain to do so and did not want him worrying about them as well. Now I have quads. The two with crystal energy keep the mermaid and the fire energy apart. That keeps their pain down. The mermaid has my grandmother's appearance. I named her such. The fire energy looks as Matt's mother and I call her that name. The pure crystal is Orvalina. The other one has my appearance and all three magic energies. I think I will call her Sam Peacemaker. Sam as she is so strong. Peacemaker as she has peace between different magic energies. Let me surprise my Matt."

Orval laughs, "Of course. Let us get you back."

I nod saying, "I want to pretend to be sleeping at first. I am tired and pretending to sleep will keep them from asking me a bunch of questions delaying my rest. I will answer their questions when I wake up."

Orval says, "Alright. You should get issues sorted out with your guardians and his guardians as soon as you can though."

I sigh, "I know. I want my babies to live. I want my Matt to live. I want to live. If I had learned Matt was fire energy before we got married, we would not be married. If I learned before our babies, they might not exist. However, if they did happen, I would have understood the pain. I did not understand it as I did not know Matt is fire magic. Sam will know though. She will never go through pain she does not understand."

Orval says, "We leave now."

I nod and close my eyes as she picks me up. Moments later, I hear a door open, then feel my Matt and his parents near. Matt asks, "Is she alright? Were you able to help her with whatever is the cause of her illness?"

Orval says, "Relax. Ann is fine now, just sleeping. You should introduce her to your mother's people as soon as possible. It is especially important that you do."

I feel her place me on the bed. Matt's father asks, "Why would that matter?"

Diana says, "If he doesn't, they might not accept her and could hurt her."

It is not could hurt me; it is they will hurt me. Nothing could cause me more pain then to lose my quads. Someone covers me up moments later. Matt says, "It is good to see you resting peacefully sweety. I am glad she was able to help you. I hope you trust me enough to share why you were ill when you wake up."

Then he kisses my forehead and dims the lights. I go to sleep. When I wake up, I head downstairs to join Matt and his parents for dinner as it is later in the day. On the way, I learn I was asleep for a couple days. Scared for my life and for my children's lives I just listen to the conversations and pick at the food I was served. I know we have to go there soon. I wonder what fire type magic Matt is. I know I will be punished for deceiving Matt however his guardians see fit. I just hope my babies and I survive it. Matt asks, "My Ann, are you feeling better?"

I answer, "I am fine. Orval was right about you, wasn't she?"

Matt answers, "Yes. Why does it matter?"

They need to know. I say, "My full name is Merth-Ann."

Diana gasps, I know she understands the issue. Matt looks confused. He does not understand. I know he would not have understood my leaving even our friendship if I had learned of his fire magic sooner. His father looks even more confused then he does. The human king has no idea what we are talking about. Matt hearing Diana gasp asks, "What?"

Diana replies, "We need to go to my parents' land now; or the protectors of the land will kill your wife."

They could and it would be their right to so to protect their magic nation. I am a threat to the entire nation at this point. Big time threat. Matt and his father ask, "Why?"

With a sigh, I state, "Because of whom I am, and that I could be a huge threat to the safety of the people. I know that I would kill anyone who was a threat to my people's safety."

Matt's father asks, "Who are you then Ann?"

Diana says, "It does not matter. We must go now. No guards as that will be taken as an act of war. We would all be killed. Without the guards we have a chance of living."

I sigh. They have a better chance then I do. Matt has about the same chance as I do as he is a threat to my entire nation. I fear for him if anything happens to me. Our children's lives are in the balance also. I tremble as we walk out to the stables. Matt's father leaving a trusted staff member in charge, a warrior.

We get in a carriage. As the carriage sets out, headed east, I go to sleep. I wake up hours later. Henry asks, "Why does your full name make a difference Ann?"

I would answer him as respect for Matt, but I need to conserve energy to protect my babies the best I can. Maybe I can save them even if I cannot save me. I go back to sleep. Every time I wake up Henry asks why my name makes a difference. I just stay quiet conserving energy. A few days later, the carriage comes to a stop. Diana says, "We will wait here."

We set up camp though it is lunch time. We are above a creator with a building in a desert down in the creator while we are in a clearing in the forest up here. There is no way down to the building that I can tell. No safe way that is.

Diana faces the creator and sits. I then understand this is the fire magic she is from. I sit beside her soon getting sleepy so lean against Diana letting sleep take over. Nothing could worsen the situation Matt and I are in. I wake up just before sunset and eat the small meal that was made for me. As the sunsets minutes after I finish eating a stranger that feels as fire magic comes over to us. He looks at Diana officially recognizing her as top rank among us and over him as he asks, "Why are you all here?"

Henry asks, "Why do you address my wife and not me?"

Understandable as most would choose to address the oldest male first. More so as he wears his crown. The male replies, "It is right that I should address my ruler before others."

Diana says, "Good. We continue on now."

I sit up. Diana stands. Matt helps me to my feet. Just a kind gesture he has no idea I need the help right now. The stranger glances at us. I saw his wondering who I am. I do not have to answer him. He called Diana his ruler meaning he is no guardian. So, I can ignore him. He leads us over to a large rock. Diana followed him so we all do. The stranger draws some symbol on the rock, and it moves revealing stairs down. I realize they lead into the creator. That is the only thing that makes since as to why Diana would face it. Matt's grip on me tightens slightly, still in a loving way.

It has been seven months since I became Matt's wife and pregnant. I place young Diana's and Mertha's conception then. Though Orvalina and Sam were conceived later, they feel the same age as their sisters. I expect all to be born in two months if I live. When we step into light in the creator with the desert scene above us and a lush valley below us that also has the building in it, Henry asks, "Diana, why is there a desert scene above us? Why are the stairs hidden?"

Silence. Henry asks, "Stranger, would you tell me?"

The stranger says something I do not understand. Henry does not seem to either as he asks, "What was that?"

Silence. Though I want to ask questions, I do not figure I have the right. Matt is just helping me down the steps. I think it is his way of dealing with the fear of losing me. He just wants to be as close to me as possible. I am glad for the help as my body is struggling to not sleep again. I do not dare if I can avoid it. Yet here in a fire energy nation, I cannot ask for energy from my people. I would not even ask the crystal people though I became their queen hours after Orval left me at home. They do not know me all that well. Henry stops asking questions. Everyone here is quiet. All the people that were here when we came in are quiet. They all feel of fire energy. I understand they are Diana's people.

We approach a large fire pit on one side of the building. On the other side of the building I saw a small pond. Oh, water. If I can make it there after my punishment ends, I might live. In the center of the large fire pit, there is a small flame. My mer magic tells me I am in danger here, to run, to stay away from this fire pit and especially the fire. Yet I have no choice. This is something I must do. I follow. The guide stops. We all stop. He steps to the side a few feet then back up until he is past Diana then pass Matt and me before he turns and walks over to six others joining them. They are the only ones standing besides Diana, Henry, Matt and me. I realize they are the council of this nation.

Diana steps into the fire pit. Matt pulls me close as I debate with myself quietly about just following her. I wait. As Diana approaches the flame in the center of the pit, the fire expands. I so want to run. Still I must let them punish me. The closer to the flame Diana gets, the bigger it gets. The fire magic council do the salute all magics do to show respect. Diana says some things I do not understand, but I am sure she is explaining the situation.

A couple minutes later, everyone of her people look shocked and scared. Mass confusion ensues. They all glance at me often and whispering. Given that, I figured they just learned I am from the mer nation. I am sorry I scare them so. I lean into Matt's side seeking comfort in what could be my last moments alive. Suddenly there is a loud command for quiet. Judging by how quickly that was obeyed, a guardian had ordered it. I look to the fire pit and see some female standing near Diana. I understand she is a guardian for this nation. She says, "We will talk with the prince and his wife."

There is no choice. We walk toward her. Diana backs away. We reach the guardian as Diana exits the fire pit. Then we are someplace new. Extremely hot here. Others are here. Only Matt and the guardian we had approached do I recognize. I realize the others are guardians also. The one who brought us here states, "Ann, Diadon says you are a mermaid, are you?"

I do not know what Diadon means but I figure it is Diana's title. I reply, "I rule the mers. I did not know Matt was a magic at all let

TALES *of the* PEACEMAKER: THE FIRST PEACEMAKER

alone a fire type. I never mentioned my magic as I thought he was human, and it is not safe to tell humans of being magic."

Matt says, "Ann, I never mentioned my magic as I thought you were human yourself. It explains why you were afraid to hear from your friend that I am fire magic. I did not understand your fear then."

I look at my feet as he does not understand fully what is at stake. The guardian said, "So you both kept your magic secret and then got married. Tell us why you also feel as a neutral type magic to us Ann."

CHAPTER THIRTY

Children

If I die, now my babies could as well. If they live, Mertha inherits the mer nation by right, and Orvalina inherits the crystal nation by right. If they die, rule reverts back to my parents and the crystal guardians would appoint the highest council member there the new ruler. To the fire guardian I reply, "On the way from the ocean to be Matt's wife I came across a female about my age. She was seriously hurt. I used my water magic to help her. When I became ill, I asked for her help. She came and took me to her home. She named me her heir. I gained neutral magic. It is why I can be here now. My water magic is in a low state now and it helps."

The guardian says, "Ann, Matt does not hear us now. Tell us are you ill for a reason, we did not attack you."

Thankful Matt does not learn of our babies this way and I can still give him the surprise I want to, provided I live, I reply, "Yes. I am with children. I feel four. One for each nation and one that has all three magic types. They are draining my energy. The fire was hurting me until I gained the neutral magic. Until I did, I only had twins. I have not told Matt yet as he was worried about me with my being in pain. I figure the mer girl and the fire girl felt threatened by each other. The other two calmed them down. I will tell Matt soon if we live."

The guardian asks, "You think we would kill you?"

I reply, "In protecting your people you would be in the right."

The guardian says, "Protecting the people would be right, but you are not a threat to them. It is clear you love Matt more then anything, except the babies. Yes, we will allow you to surprise him. The dragon child is able to rule here and so is the one with all three energies. Pure dragon will rule here. The three-magic child will have authority over her, but I think it would hurt her mer abilities to stay here. She should stay with you."

Then before I can say anything else, this guardian, Matt and I are back in the fire pit. The guardian says, "We accept this union."

They must have released Matt's hearing because he excited says, "Accepted."

Matt spins me slightly before hugging me slightly tight and kissing me. I enjoy it but I need air for our babies. I push him back saying, "Matt please. Our babies need air."

As expected, he is surprised. Then excitement takes over. He asks, "Babies, as in more than one?"

I reply, "As in quads. There are four."

Matt looks me over then asks, "How far along are you?"

I laugh, "I became pregnant the night we were married. Mers do not show until they are starting the ninth month along. The babies are why I am so tired all the time. I was in pain as one is a complete dragon and one is a complete mer. They were scared of each other. The other two calmed them down."

Matt says, "When were you going to tell me?"

I say, "Originally I was planning on your birthday, but I slept clear through it. Then you were worried about my health and I did not want to increase your worry, so I decided to wait until I was not stressing you. After that I was not sure if any of us would live so I waited. Now we only have to talk to my guardians."

Matt becomes sad. He says, "They could end my life."

I shake my head, saying, "No Matt, they cannot. I would protect you. I would hurt for a while if we lose our babies, but I would die if anything happened to you. I just need to tell them what happened since I left the mer nation. Our babies are innocents. They will not be harmed."

Taking his hand, I lead him over to the pond knowing my guardians would know it as soon as I touch the water. I am holding his hand with the one my mer symbol is on the wrist of. It is so small not even magics can read what it says, at least no magic I have currently came across. Still holding his hand, I use that hand to touch the water as I say in mer royal language, "Mer guardians I know you are strong enough to know what I say. I am safe. I am in a fire magic land as my husband is fire magic, a dragon. The guardians here have accepted our union. I am with child. More than one. I feel different as I gained crystal magic, it is a neutral type. Do you accept our union?"

The pond ripples then mer words appear. The words read as "Crazy child for marrying a fire magic. However, there is no retraction of our acceptance of your marriage, glad you are and will be safe. Come to the nation before your children are born."

I say in magic common, "Thank you guardians."

Then I face Matt and say, "They accept us. I just have to go to the mer nation before our children are born. Chances are they will be born there. That is not something we have say in. My people do not know they exist. The crystals do as Orval told them. The dragons just heard it, but my people do not know. It will be difficult to adjust to pressure differences while pregnant. Once they are born, I could make the trip easier. Remember I saw you every other day while we were just starting our friendship. I made the trip upriver in two hours to the point you led me through the forest to. Downstream to the ocean's depths took me an hour. My culture revolves around sea life because I am a part of the sea life."

Matt laughs. Then asks, "Mom says that she originally thought of having you wear a high slit or low V-neck dress, but you refused. Any reason for that?"

I reply, "My mer marking. I have one that covers my upper chest, wraps around my body and ends on my thigh. I did not want anyone seeing it. Besides that, only you get right to see my body."

Matt says, "Funny, but I never saw the mark."

I say, "I had my guardians suppress it, until after I had told you about my being a mer. I had worked up the courage to show you then we had argued. I guess you did not realize I could keep you safe. I can breathe air and water. I breathe out air when I breathe in water. I was intending to help you and show you where I am from. I am to far along in my pregnancy to do that now. Maybe later. I cannot even change into a mer yet because as soon as I do my nation's calling will get strong enough to take me back there until they are born."

Matt understands. While we were talking I hear Diana tell Henry about us going to the guardian space, that everyone listened to the woman as she had learned how to live forever and achieved it, that she had explained to everyone who I was, and that the flame grows for the royals of the nation. She also mentions she was not sure how to mention this place as many have attacked her people, the desert scene helps her people stay safe, that everyone stills when an immortal talks so to hear and follow any instructions in hope of learning how to live forever, and that the language was her native language; the language of this place.

At that moment, a dragon flies in and becomes a young girl. Henry looks ready to attack the child. Diana moves between them just as fast as I process that. I understand Henry has no idea he married any dragon let alone their ruler. Diana says, "You do not want to try to harm anyone here, I will protect my people."

Henry asks, "What do you mean?"

Diana replies, "I am a dragon, their king, we have no word for queen, and our son is a dragon too. We will protect the dragons from any threat."

With her words I understand that young Diana and Sam will both one day be called king. Strange to me but it is their ways and I will accept that. Henry asks, "*Merth-Ann* is she a dragon too?"

Diana replies, "Not a dragon; a mermaid. If she had been a dragon it would not have been necessary to bring her to meet everyone."

That is right. They would have known me. I would have had to pass the council test to marry the nation's heir. However, Diana and the dragons need to know I am not just a mermaid. I say, "Queen; I am the queen of the Mers, not just a mermaid."

Diana says, "That explains how come you are strong enough to survive."

I know. I doubt any of my people would have been able to handle it. Diana tells Henry all magic common laws and further explains why she does not talk about this place. After he understands it all, we go back to his nation.

....

We had been gone a week. Henry says nothing about any of our magic. He just tells his people that we had meant with Diana's people, the marriage had been accepted and then we came back here. Then Henry makes magic common laws part of his nation's laws. I knew he was a good man. He helped raise my Matt after all.

That evening, alone in our quarters Matt asks, "Can I see you as a mer?"

I nod asking, "Do I get to see you as a dragon?"

Matt replies, "Sure."

He shows me his dragon looks. Pure bright purple scales larger than mine. His wings are silver. Knowing it is my Matt, I find I think of that dragon as yum too. Would I have if I did not know it was him? I do not know. Matt changes back saying, "Mom and I are the only purple dragons. Her color is darker than mine. I am nearly certain our dragon baby is a shade of purple also."

I say, "Mer royals are purple as well. Crystal royals are purple tented white. Yes, all four have a shade of purple for their aura."

Matt says, "Mermaid?"

I walk into the bathroom and fill the tub. Matt has followed me. I get in fully dressed and relax. In moments, my legs vanish, and my tail appears. I lean back saying, "Maybe later we could go swimming alone in the ocean Matt. Just the two of us. Well from here anyways. We could come across some wateries or some mers. Especially if I show you where I grew up."

Matt says, "Sounds good. Would I get to meet your parents?"

Changing back to human appearance and getting out of the tub, I reply, "Sure."

Matt says, "You are extremely attractive to me. Both ways. I drew your image the day we met, even without knowing your name. I wanted you even then. I regretted not asking you for your name when I did not figure ever seeing you again."

I say, "I wanted you that long too. You are so yum to me. I mean everything about you appeals to me. Even your dragon looks now that I have seen them. The guardians were my first true friends, they treated me without the respect my people did. Martha was my first mortal friend. Her extreme need for help made me respond when I hid from most until I could learn about them. She helped me learn about the human's language, that is common here and what different terms mean. She helped me learn what is able to be eaten. Things such as yeast, she could not explain what are and I avoid them because I do not know. She joined the mer nation so she could live there easier. After she did that, our friendship was strained as I was in authority over her. You were my next true friend. Your helping me when I was so in need made a lasting impact in my mind. I have a few friends now. None know I am a mer. They do not even know I am a royal. In the first few weeks after you helped me, I referred to you as Mr. Yum. Say something!"

Instead of saying anything, Matt kisses me deeply. Yum. I respond by wrapping my arms around him. Then Matt asks, "Still want me to talk?"

I mutter, "What do we need to talk about? Yummy. I am glad you love me."

Matt says, "I am the lucky one. I got you, fish girl."

I giggle, "That is fish queen. I rule after all. You just call me love, Ann or beautiful. Then again I do not mind you calling me my fish."

Matt laughs. I go to sleep leaning against his chest. A month later, at dinner, I say, "It is time I go see how my people are doing. I need to ensure their safety. Are you fine with my going there?"

They nod. Matt walks me to the river before telling me to be safe and make sure our babies were safe also. I say, "Of course Matt, see you as soon as I can. I will get a shell etching done of them after their birth so you can have it."

Matt says, "Sounds good. The sea awaits. Come home soon."

I look around making sure we were alone then walk into the river. Lower myself to the water height and swim downstream as a human. By the time I reach the ocean twenty minutes later, I am exhausted. I say, "Wela, please help me get to my nation."

Wela comes over to me asking, "What is wrong Ann? I have seen you swim that distance many times easily, yet now you tire?"

I reply, "As if you do not know. I am pregnant. Please help me."

Wela asks, "Are you having a son or a daughter?"

I state, "Daughters."

Wela gasps, "You pluralized it. Twins."

I state, "No. Quads. I am having four."

Wela says, "You are joking right?"

I yawn. Wela asks, "Can I stay for their birth?"

Sleepy, I mutter, "Um hum."

Wela holds me as she moves down. Seeing my thinking space seconds later, I say, "There please for a moment."

So, she takes me there. Tark shoots his water ball at us. I am too weak to deflect it. Thankfully, Wela steps in front of me and absorbs it. Meme shows up and calms Tark down before saying, "Dangerous to come here with your babies Ann. I am sure you understand the reason that is."

I say, "Diana and Sam."

Meme says, "The one yes. The other is a mer. Not sure which one is which."

I say, "I just wanted to thank the guardians again for accepting my union to my Matt. I could not live without him anymore. I could not. We argued once. I nearly killed myself from that. It was when I was going to tell him about my being a mer. I scared him. He reacted in that fear. We argued and I tried to kill myself. He prevented my urchin from doing as I had ordered it to dry me out completely then he assured me he loved me and explained I had made him think I was trying to end his life. He understands now I was going to show him the mer nation."

Meme says, "Go there. They need to know you are pregnant. By the way, you are starting to show."

I say, "Oh, beautiful… Wela, please."

Wela helps me to my city. In moments Janice is near us asking, "What happened?"

Grinning Wela says, "Look closer healer. Your Queen is pregnant."

Janice looks at me again then smiles, "Of course! What is the baby's name?"

I say, "My parents should have been at my wedding. They would have enjoyed meeting my husband and his parents. I am glad they accept my union to him and accept him into their family. I wonder…."

Healer says, "Pardon Queen, but wonder what?"

I say, "Library first Janice. I need the ruler's staff."

We go to the library then to the throne room. There I call for a national meeting. In minutes, every mer is in their normal seats here. It is quiet as they all wait for me to talk. I say, "Martha, thank you for helping me know how to behave and talk on the land so I could pass as one of them. As everyone knows, I left here to get married to one I love and live with him. His name is Matt. That was eight months ago. I return a bit earlier then I had expected to as I am eight months pregnant."

As I pause to catch my breath and keep my energy up, they all congratulate me on my baby. To that, I shake my head saying, "Not baby. Babies. I am having quads. Four daughters."

I see everyone's extreme shock. I understand it as no magic has ever had more then two that any magic knows about. I was stunned to feel twins at first. Equally stunned when the other two came to be. I continue, "I named the pure mer maiden Mertha after my grandmother. After she is three days old, she becomes your queen, so you all do not have to worry if your queen is safe. Martha can raise her with help from my parents, the council and the guardians. Know that once she is five, she will come visit her family where I live now for a few days every year. She will be here most of the time, but I need to see her too. I think her being your queen is best for all of us. I do wish to bring my Matt here and let him learn about how I grew up. On the way to become Matt's wife I help the queen of the crystals. She named me her heir. When she died, I became their queen as well. It is fitting then that the pure crystal girl is named after her. I call that baby Orvalina. My friend was named Orval. Something that she said before taking me to meet her people explained the massive pain I was in at the time. She was right. My Matt is fire energy. He is the dragon prince."

Mass confusion and fear run around. I command, "Calm down!"

Instant quiet though they are all still not calm by any means. I continue, "I had the same reaction you all just did. Mine was worse as I was concerned for my life, my babies' lives, and Matt's life. The guardian of all nations involved accept our union. I named the pure dragon girl after Matt's mother Diana. She has her looks as well, except my eye color instead of the red color Matt's mother has. She will one day be king of the dragons as they have no word for queen."

As I pause to let them absorb all that information, someone asks, "What about your fourth baby?"

I reply, "Her name is Sam Peacemaker. Sam has all three energies, my appearance and right to rule over all her siblings. She cannot live in any of the magic nations she inherited skills off of or lose skills from the others. Therefore, she has to live with Matt and me in the human nation. Yes, I understand the dangers that causes for her, but I am sure she will be able to pass off being human to the humans. After all Matt and I both thought each other was human. We would not have gotten married if we suspected otherwise. I wanted to let you all know before their birth. I also promised my Matt he would get an etching of the four of them together. Orvalina and Diana will be placed in their magic nations after I leave here. I am very tired now, good night."

Yawning I walk out. Janice, Martha and my parents are quick to follow me. Martha asks, "Why do you honor me so?"

Reaching the library, I once again leave the staff there with the other ruling items. I reply, "You are my friend. One of the very few I have. The guardians, the council, you, Matt, and a few others are all that treat me as friends. The guardians I show the same respect to that my people show to me. Even if they do not enjoy it, I do not know how else to act. The council talks to me about things in the nation but as their clan's leader it is partly their job to do so, to ensure their clan has needs and issues taken care of. You are the first one that treated me as a friend."

Martha says, "You saved my life. I was a stranger and you saved my life."

I reply, "Your information has saved me many times. It continues to serve me and help me remain hidden among the humans. I just saw Matt looking as a dragon a month before I came here. That is when he saw me as a mer. Mom, were you excited to have me?"

Mom replies, "Yes. When I told your father, I was expecting to have his baby, I thought he could have jumped clear out of the ocean in one leap. It only added to my happiness."

I laugh, "Matt seemed grounded which was the calm I needed after the stress of needing the approval of his guardians and mine. I was nearly sure Meme and her equals would not retract their acceptance of a union and I am glad they did not, still I had to ask. It was the guardians Matt falls under that I was stressed the most about. I mean I had unknowingly joined their people and I am not even that energy type. I was a threat and I knew it. They accepted us. Then I knew I was safe, so I told Matt about our babies. I had planned on doing so earlier, but I slept through his birthday and then he was stressed because I was in pain and tired a lot and he did not know the reason. I did not want to add to that stress. I knew the tiredness was expected but the pain I had was far greater than anything recorded in the archives. I could not figure out why so much pain. I figured the mers before me had downplayed the pain so others would not avoid having babies. I realize now they did not. Of course, fire and water babies in a confined space would feel threatened by each other. Orvalina and Sam stay between Mertha and Diana. The pain now is at the level I read about."

Then I lean against a wall in the castle. My eyes are nearly shut. Janice says, "Get some rest Queen, your mother and I can get you to your room."

I say, "I am sure you both could. I just want to walk there on my own if I can."

Dad says, "Do not over do yourself Ann. Pregnancy certainly took a lot from your mother and she only had you."

I say, "I am sure. However, I am still alert and intend to walk."

Five minutes later, we approach my quarters and I am getting drowsy. We go into my sitting area. I stretch out on the couch.

Soon my eyes close. I am in the forest around the dragon area. I do not know how I got here. I see dragons fly overhead. Many green dragons, red dragons, brown dragons, white dragons, and black dragons. Only three purple dragons and one rainbow dragon. I follow that one curious as to why it is different. Suddenly I am on the crystal world. It is how I saw it when I was there except there is a rainbow crystal now. I move toward it wondering how it came to be so different. Then I am in the great room here sitting by my parents at our personal table. My daughter Mertha is sitting with us as Sam is on the throne. Then Sam goes for a swim and I see she has a rainbow-colored tail. Well that explains everything. Sam is incredibly unique. Her items and appearances would be too. I wake up in my quarters still pregnant. Was that a dream? If not, what was it? If it was, what just occurred because I feel as if it is fact.

Janice asks, "How do you feel?"

I question, "Why are you asking?"

Janice says, "You were asleep three weeks. How do you feel?"

I say, "It was so real."

Janice asks, "Queen?"

I reply, "My dream. It was so real."

Then I hear Meme command, "Out! I will talk alone with Ann."

We are left alone. Meme sits by me. I go to sit up and she places her hand on my chest saying, "Relax. That was not just a dream Ann. Sam is rainbow-colored. You saw future events. At least boss said you had activated his time spear and the images you saw were shown. We all want to know how you did it? It is entirely under boss's control, yet you managed to use it. How did you do so?"

I state, "I am not even sure what you talk about. Sam seems to be different though. As if nothing is wrong. As if her sisters were not drained. As if I was not tired. Why is she so alert when none of her siblings or I have energy?"

Zeffron shows up saying, "Interesting. My energy spear lit up and it is focused here. Yet you have no extra energy. Are you sure it is Sam?"

I say, "What are you talking about? Sam is more alert then I am. That is all I am sure of."

Zeffron says, "Sam are you using my spears?"

I hear myself ask, "How would I know how to? Am I that special?"

Then I wonder why I answered a question guardian asked my daughter. I wonder why guardian asked when Sam is not born yet. Meme says, "Ann when a magic is not born but is asked a question, their mother answers what they would have. It is the mother's voice to the child's words. Do you understand?"

I reply, "I expect as much as any could without being an immortal."

Zeffron says, "Sam, did you use my things? Yes or no."

Sam replies, "Ask your boss's child if you can find that one."

Next that I know I am waking up to Janice telling me I was asleep for five days. I could give birth at any time. Mom and Janice help me up. We go to the gathering room. Minutes later, all mers are gathered. They witness the birth of my quads. Diana is born first as she is the weakest in this environment. Then Orvalina is born. Followed by Mertha. Finally, Sam is born. None of my people can draw anyone except Mertha. Nothing else seems right. After I rejected all the attempts done, Sam changes appearance of age and says, "Mom, they cannot draw people they do not know the symbols of. Let me. I will show you my symbol."

I nod. Sam takes the coral sheet and etches in Mertha fully. It is so good I could almost believe it is alive. After Sam shows everyone, and many mers comment about the strong resemblance Sam etches Orvalina a bit away from the etching of Mertha. It also looks nearly alive. Many mers comment about the strong resemblance. Then Sam etches Diana making a triangle with the etchings. That also looks nearly alive. Sam etches in each of their symbols beside them on the inside of the triangle. I see her connect the symbols with a circle saying, "I am Sam Peacemaker. This is my symbol and my looks."

Sam then hands it to me saying, "A gift for my parents."

I look and all four etchings appear nearly alive. I see Sam's symbol is the three nations in a triangle on a circle. Sam's image is in the center. Her sisters are on the outside. I smile at the resemblance, I say, "Thank you Sam. It looks so real."

Sam says, "It fades. The image needs traced by the one of each nation that raises my sisters. You chose Martha to raise Mertha. She should trace the etching with a scale from Mertha. That will make it last."

I get a scale off of Mertha, hand it to Martha with the etchings and have her trace the etching of her princess. She does so then places Mertha's scale back on her. Mertha touches her smiling.

Three days later, I officially turn overrule to Mertha put my other three into a carrier and travel to the crystal nation. There I have the woman of a strong couple trace the etching of Orvalina using a bit of Orvalina's crystal before asking the couple to raise her and turning overrule of the crystals to my daughter. I let them all know that Orvalina will visit her family once a year as soon as she turns five. They understand. The couple I asked to raise Orvalina ask why I honored them so to give them the responsibility of caring for their young queen. I state, "You are strong and kind. She needs that. Could have been anyone. You are the first couple I saw with strength outside of the council. I am sure they will help you teach her to be good for the nation. The guardians also. I need to go take the little dragon to her home now. Bye. I will not be back."

They nod. I leave. From there I go to the dragon nation. The people are slightly nervous around me. I say, "I just bring my dragon babies here."

The guardian I saw last time says, "Bring Sam and Diana Diadon here."

I obey asking, "What does that mean?"

The guardian says, "Diadon is the last name of the dragon ruler. We call the nation's heir Dia. Sam is over Diana but Diana rules here. Only the council as a whole could raise Diana for you. Anything you want to say before you leave with Sam?"

I reply, "Diadon Diana will visit her sisters in the land that I now live when she is five and older once a year. I will not come here. I do request that someone that will help raise Diana use one of her scales to trace an etching I had done of her so Matt can see how his daughters look. It is starting to fade, and I was told that doing as I asked would make it last."

The guardian does that herself. Then asks me to leave and not come back without Diana having invited me. I do so carrying Sam with me. Yet I know it is extremely dangerous for a magic to live with humans. Especially one so different then any one magic. It just has to be. I think over how to make sure Sam stays safe as I walk home. A few hours later I am in the forest when the tigers surround me. They smell the air then one approaches me alone. Nervous I slowly sit down holding out my arms slightly, I say, "This is Sam. She is Matt's and my daughter."

The tiger closest to me licks Sam. Sam coos. I relax slightly as Sam enjoys the contact. The tigers walk off. I stand up, hide Sam again and walk back into the nation that is home now. I go to the castle nodding to whoever speaks to me. Mostly they say, "Princess, Sire Matt will be glad you are back."

I know it. I am glad to be back. Unknown to the people I have one of my four babies with me. They will only know of her unless they are magic. I enter the castle, mentally rejecting anyone who bows to me and go directly to Matt in our quarters. Matt's whole expression lights up on seeing me. I smile glad to be home. Then I rock side to side slightly causing Sam to coo. Matt beams, "Is that our youth?"

Laughing, I close the door before I reply, "This is Sam. She is our daughter, it is dangerous for her because of her heritage. She needs to be allowed to fight, so she can protect herself without showing any of her magic."

Then I hand him the etchings and say, "Sam did it. Someone from each nation traced the etchings to make them last. Told you their names already. I had them a month after I left. That was a few days ago. Let us take care of Sam."

Matt says, "Come on."

We go to his parents' quarters and meet alone with them. Matt explains what I had told him. An hour later, Henry calls a national meeting. He announces that I had a daughter, that any female can fight, and reserves the names Sam and Samantha for the royal family. He also says that the names can be used by either gender before he introduces Sam as his heir stating that she would rule once she was eighteen or if he died and she was at least eight. I see people come forward and request to change their names. They were all called Sam or Samantha. I am shocked at how much respect this human gets. Then I hear Mertha, Orvalina and Diana order the names Sam and Samantha removed from use in their nations reserving them for the Peacemaker's family line as Sam is their king. It shocks me but I learned to hide shock well and no one notices.

Henry then changes the symbol of his nation to match Sam's symbol and changes the nation's name to Peacemaker, officially making it her last name. Now only she can rule after Henry. If they even respect Sam as much as they do Henry everything will turn out good for her. I know she will be able to earn their respect now. Then later if they learn of her magic, they would not try to harm her as she would have proven she can be trusted to them. In the meantime, Henry is protective enough of Diana, Matt, me and Sam that we are safe. Henry is that protective of his friends as well. I am once again reminded how good of a nation I came into such a short time ago. I wonder what adventures my children will have but that is for another story. You have learned how the first Peacemaker came to be.

Lightning Source UK Ltd.
Milton Keynes UK
UKHW010637280521
384539UK00001B/148